Deadly Secret

Deadly Secret

James W. Roberts Sr.

Copyright @ 2008 by James W. Roberts Sr.

Written by James W. Roberts Sr.

ISBN   978-0-615-26324-3   Softcover

This Novel was printed in the United States of America.

To order additional copies of this book contact
 Lulu Markets or contact publisher
1-706- 335-7955

Dedication

Mom and Dad this one is for you
In loving memory of my Mom and Dad
Ruth Evelyn (Byrd) Roberts
Glenn Dayton Roberts

Introduction

Deadly Secret

James W. Roberts Sr.

 Growing up in a place, having found memories that seems never to be out of fashion is what reminded me of a couple of young men I once knew in my collage years, my room mate Daryl told a pretty old fashioned store of when Boy meets girl, when they become sweethearts and how it completely changes ones life.
 The story he told of his first meeting a girl called Leona seemed to last for days and I never realized it might be one of the best stories I had ever heard.
The other young man called Terry was a go getter type of guy who seemed to want it all and in Collage he pretty much had his way, he is another story that had to be told in due time .
 Two men young men that passed each others paths in the walk of life that left an old fashion memory deep in my mind, a story I tell from time to time as my years goes quietly into the ages.

Deadly Secret

James W. Roberts Sr.

Ellisville, West Virginia is a beautiful mountain town a small metropolitan full of spring flowers and the hint of the past winter in the air, this town has it all, captivating   views that would be pleasing to any eye.

There are ski slopes near by ready for the tourist to discover, trout streams flowing with cool crisp waters stocked with trout year round and waterfalls to gaze upon with delightful surrounding views.

Scenic hunting lodges for those who have the call of the wild both private and public with wild game a plenty, Bear, Deer, and Pheasant, to name a few, along with a place to kick back and absorb all the tranquility it has to offer.

There are enormous caves waiting to be discovered and explored.

Rapids for kayaking and canoeing, mountain lakes so high you would think you were in heaven going on a fishing trip, the summers are lazy days getting away from everyday life's routine of things, the time for picnics, barbeques, camping, water skiing and doing absolutely nothing.

Paradise in the mountains, people are naturally haunted by all her majesty of all consuming appeal.

In this mountain range was a place where notorious men had visited and enjoyed.

People of all walks of life has either visited her or decided to stay, no matter where in the United States one could go, there never will be a state more beautiful than her, the one God has crafted in his finest landscaping that couldn't be copied.

The place where Daryl Moonie talks about when he and his wife goes on vacation, no one would have ever thought he was a chemistry teacher, a tour guide maybe, with the build up he gave his home town which is in the spectacular, incredible Mountain grandeur "West Virginia!"

It was the first week in August, school was beginning in Ellisville and several seniors were standing in the front of the Ellisville Comprehensive High School, they saw Mr. Moonie pulling up in the parking lot of the school as he had done so many times in previous years.

Daryl normally was the first to arrive at school and the first to leave. This was Daryl Moonies and his wife Leona's fourteenth wedding anniversary and he wasn't in all that big of a hurry to leave home that morning, he wanted the day to start out special for his wife and it wouldn't have mattered to him if he were late.

He was looking forward to teaching the seniors this year, it was something about adding some more fine tuning to their intellect that energized Daryl, it seemed the young adults were getting smarter every year and they would challenge him at every opportunity.

Darrel had went to his locker in the teachers lounge poured a cup of coffee looking over some papers and noticed a letter from an old collage friend he hadn't seen in years, when he opens the letter it actually wasn't from his friend.

Daryl looked at the envelope seeing he had misread the name, it was from his brother Phil telling him about his brother Terry whom was Daryl's friend and told him about Terry's wife dieing and thought he would like to know.

It saddens Daryl to hear about his friends' wife and decided to give him a call, his friend was a teacher in Glendale, New Mexico and he called the school to give his condolences to his friend.

Daryl waited on him to come to the phone for about five minutes, he knew sometimes things could be very busy early in the morning at a school, but if he didn't come to the phone right away he knew he would have to call some other time.

Daryl only had about six minutes until his class would start.

Just as he started to hang up he heard a voice say Daryl and he spoke to the person saying yes this is Daryl Moonie and the strangest thing accrued he was disconnected, he looked at his watch then hurried to his class room.

Daryl was stopped outside of the teacher's lounge that was the beginning of Daryl's nightmare, being put into a situation where his choices were limited and would forever change the lives of all who knew him.

Everyone has some sort of history and Daryl's starts way before he was born.

Lets go back and take a look at his and his wife's history after all once they were married they became one and actually the story is as much about her as it is him, maybe more so.

What is it that makes people want to search for a place to live somewhere besides the place they were born, could it be kismet, this question lies on the minds of a lot of people when there young one moves away from home.

Who would ever thought Ellisville, West Virginia would have a background in its history of notorious men, it seems all over West Virginia there was something going on all the time.

A mixture of truth and folklore no matter what the story was there was someone giving there version of it and more times than not the story got bigger and bigger or side tracked from time to time,

Did you ever hear about the feud of the Hatfield's and the McCoy's? According to folklore that may be pretty close to the way the events happened, theses two families Hatfield's and McCoy's.

They were prominent good ole boys and gals who lived along the Kentucky-West Virginia border, on opposite sides of a stream known as Tug Fork, off the Big Sandy River.

Both clans were part of the first band of squatters to settle the Tug Valley.

The McCoy's, was led by an old timer whose name was Randolph, "Randal" for short McCoy and lived on the Kentucky side of the river, while the Hatfield's, led by another old timer by the name of William Anderson nick named" Devil Anse" Hatfield that occupied the West Virginia side.

It seems the governor, a well loved man by the Hatfield's would chose to be their mediator, the governor of West Virginia, E. Willis Wilson, accused Kentucky of violating the extradition process.

Now you know he had just stuck his head in a noose, he claimed Kentucky kidnapped the Hatfield's and appealed the matter all the way to the Supreme Court of the United States.

It would be fair to say it was conclusive that in May of 1889, the Supreme Court ruled against West Virginia and the Hatfield's stood trial in Kentucky and all eight Hatfield's were found guilty of murder.

It was told that the governor was furious when one of them was publicly hanged for the murder of Alifair McCoy, the daughter of Randel McCoy who was killed in January 1888 on the raid of his home and the other seven were sentenced to life in prison.

Well this is a fact look it up.

Some say West Virginians keep things all to themselves, actually they don't, they will be glad to share their heritage with you, just ask them if they have had Indians, Gunslingers, prostitutes, millionaires, derelicts, bootleggers, Union Soldiers, Confederates Soldiers, bank robbers, buggy wrecks and most of all tales of mysterious deaths. Try to say all that in one breath.

Not the kind of history one would suspect of such a well known town, the kind of mixture that breeds the finniest stock of people on earth, the kind of people that doesn't spread gossip.

They just start it.

This robust place that's forged its way through time and is in the heart of all whom live there, because of being one of America's finniest places to raise children, this is some of the history of this town and the people are proud of its heritage, there is no shame in telling the story.

It's funny what attracts people to certain towns, the heritage of this town was past down through the generations it may have got a little mixed up along the way, but who hasn't.

It is this kind of heritage that bought two men into Ellisville with their wives in 1934, both men like the true stories they read about Kid Curry and wild Bill Cody and also the stories of the Hatfield's and McCoy's.

Harvey Logan, (1867 - June 17, 1904) also known as Kid Curry, was a notorious outlaw and gunman who ran with Butch Cassidy and the Sundance Kid's infamous Wild Bunch gang.

Not to be spreading rumors but some say Senator Elkins of West Virginia once was thought to be Jessie James wouldn't that have been a hoot, we could finally say any one can be a senator.

It has been told Kid Curry was responsible for the killing of at least nine law enforcement officers in five or six different shootings, and a couple other men in other instances, as well as having several shootouts wile he was being chased by posses.

It even has been said he killed a few civilians during his outlaw days.

There are stories he stayed up in the hills of West Virginia for a while left and ended up in jail down in Knoxville Tennessee but he escaped on the mayor's horse or at least that's the way rumor has it.

Some say Wild Bill Cody was one of the most colorful figures of the Old west and became a pretty good spokesman for what was called the New West.

He was born William Frederick Cody in Iowa in 1846.

When he was nick named "Buffalo Bill" it was somewhere in Kansas if memory serves he was 22.

He had been a trapper, a Pony Express rider, some say a wagon master, stagecoach driver and ran a Wild West show, to name a few hats he wore, he earned his nickname for his skill while supplying pacific railroad workers with buffalo meat and some tell that some Indians just about starved because of it.

There is stories he killed all the buffalo in West Virginia, and traded it to the Seneca Indians for salt to take west, it has been suggested he even wore the mow hawk hair style for a while until he had gotten frost bit in Death Valley while he was crossing the desert at night.

In his Wild West show he introduced Sitting Bull a Famous War Chief at little Big Horn Massacre.

Sitting Bull was victorious in the Battle of Little Bighorn where General George Armstrong Custer and the 76th Cavalry Regiment launched an early dawn attack against a Native American camp.

What Custer did not know was that Sitting Bull had gained a great deal of support and had fortified several of the Native American camps in the area.

Could it be it was the excitement of living where notorious men had walked the streets of a place in the upper south east that had as much as a western spirit as any town in the west?

Who would ever think these men traveled around in the Mountain State of West Virginia, not knowing where they were most of the time thinking they were some where in Kentucky.

The people in Ellisville were pioneers in every since of the word, molding out a way of life that would forever change the way people would look at the west of being the only place in history of having notorious men.

John Moonie and Brent Martin were complete strangers but never the less arrived in Ellisville because of the same attraction to this Wild West presentation that was in the upper south east.

Moonie lived on the east side of Ellisville at one thirty eight Belmont Street and Martin leaved on the south side in a royal area, Moonie came to Ellisville to work as a DJ, he hope to open the first radio broadcasting station in Ellisville.

But Moonie would find out in a hurry there wasn't to many interested of having that kind of business in this town at this particular time, in order for him to support his wife he started working with a group of carpenters.

They were building a local church and he stayed working with this group until 1936, a conglomerate of business men decided it was time for Ellisville to have a broadcasting system and Moonie went to work for this new radio station BNOX.

A station that's becoming well know and was broadcasted out of a well known lodge called the Cheat River Lodge in which he moved in to a room with his wife and paid an outstanding cost of a dollar a week to live there.

In the same year his wife gave birth to a son giving him the name Daryl.

John Moonies dad had a law firm in Buffalo, New York and hoped his son would walk in his foot steps; it broke his heart that his son pulled up stakes and moved to Ellisville, but would later have his way when John realized his dream could never support his family.

John was still leaving on an allowance given to him by his father, the twelve dollars a week he was paid; he couldn't afford the things his family should have.

John swallowed his pride and allowed his dad to set him up in law practice in Ellisville after John refused to go back to New York; John made a good living, built a beautiful home for his wife and son then lived a very happy life in Ellisville.

His family name became well known to all in the town, a name that was looked upon with honor and respect, he mostly handled clients from the upper part of Ellisville so he would actually get paid.

A chicken or a bag of flour for his services wouldn't pay his bills.

His son Daryl at age ten would spend a lot of time with his grand parents who bought a farm right out side of Ellisville in a town called Elkins, named after Senator Elkins; Elkins was born near New Lexington, Ohio.

He moved with his family to Westport, Missouri (now part of Kansas City) in the mid-1840s to Philip Duncan Elkins and Sarah Pickett Withers.

He attended the Masonic College in Lexington, Missouri in the 1850s, and graduated from the University of Missouri in Columbia in 1860.

After graduation, he briefly taught school in Cass County, Missouri. Among his pupils was future James Younger Gang member Cole Younger, it was said these young men rode with Jesse James.

His grandfather had retired moved to Elkins bought a farm on Chenoweth Creek Road, Daryl loved this farm and he had his secret place, that's what he would tell his grand parents.

Daryl would go there to play with his toy solider and read the jokes on the back of bubble gun wrappers, he would play marbles with some neighboring kids and came home one day and showed his grandmother a huge marble he won, called a cat eye.

This was one of Daryl's most valuable items he kept hid, his grand parents knew where his secret place was and they were delighted to see him go there.

It was one place he could be himself and be like the pirates in his favorite books, Daryl could hide his treasures like the pirates and disclose his hiding place to those of his choosing.

Daryl used his street address to disclose how to find his treasure in his hiding place, his grand father passed away when he was twelve and left him a considerable amount of money and put it in a trust fund for him.

Daryl couldn't receive his money until his twenty fifth birth day and then he could spend it any way he liked, most kids would be exhilarated over receiving an inheritance, Daryl might have been too if he knew exactly what it was, he was told he had a nest egg to look forward to and he didn't think there was any need of him having a nest with eggs in it.

Daryl wasn't the type where money meant a whole lot, even though he found it handy to have on occasions, but at his age visiting his relatives was what he enjoyed most or at least some of them.

Daryl like going to his aunts while his Uncle Bingaman was alive, His uncle was a bee keeper, who sold honey to help with expenses after his retirement from the post office, but passed away when Daryl was nine.

His aunt was a busy body, Daryl didn't care too much for her and she sold all the bee hives except one that she had placed on her front porch so Daryl would still come visit her.

He might not have liked her but she was family and everyone has their quirks, come to think of it she did make a wonderful chocolate cake so all and all she was ok to him only if she wouldn't talk about other members of the family.

Daryl realized it was the young folk whom liked her, one could say the only thing she had going for her was the children all the adults would avoid her, but Darryl sure like pretending.

So for a few years he hung out on her porch pretending he was a bee keeper.

Daryl loved building things, a dog house was his first project that he completed by himself and at a very young age became a quite remarkable craftsman.

When he was sixteen he built a desk for his dad not telling anyone of the secret it had, which was two drawers that locked from behind making them look fake to anyone who would try to open them and he had the only key.

It made Daryl remember what his grandfather had told him, about a bible verse from Matthew 6:3 that he quoted like a cliché not to allow the left hand to know what the right hand was up to.

Although the scripture was talking about giving alms in a private manner, Daryl took his grandfathers figure of speech to heart and made this a way of life, on the other side of town lived Brent Martin.

He took Ellisville by storm he was a salesman and he could sale refrigerators to Eskimos if he had a mind to, he went to work for the Bramble Co. a supplier of commercial doors, frames and Hardware fixtures.

He made a remarkable salary of seventy five dollars a week something that not too many people had the privilege of earning, in witch his employers thought was cheap.

Mr. Bramble had commented if they paid him twice that amount they still would come out ahead, from the amount of sales Martin had made for this company made them the largest supplier in the upper south east, it wasn't long before the company was giving him a full partnership.

His wife gave birth to two children, Leona and Jerry who carried on a tradition of sibling rivalry, Brent and his wife was a very happy couple.

These two who enjoyed spending time with their children, they liked the quite life and the bond the family had would allow them to go through many difficulties in life and were made stronger because of it.

No matter how angry they got at each other they never held a grudge and would make up shortly after they had an argument, like a lot of families they always used the cliché blood is thicker than water only this family really knew what it meant.

Unconditional love no one needs to say more.

Leona was full of life, a beautiful girl, smart, which was very out going around her parents, but was somewhat reserved around other people thinking it wasn't appropriate for a young girl to be the center of attention.

Once she set her eye on something she would want to do, she was like a bull dog that would grab holds not turn lose and it would seem Jerry could always bring the worst out in her.

Jerry like most brothers like tormenting her, by teasing her, calling her names and pulling her hair, he was a pain at times, although at times he could be her best friend.

This skinny little boy actually loved his sister, but he often would try to bully her, they had been in the yard playing when Jerry thought it was time he would show her who head knight of their castle was.

Jerry told her he was Sir Lancelot and she was the enemy of the king because of her dragon face, laughing at her Jerry walked up to her pretended to slap her face then smiled and challenged her to a duel.

Understand Jerry was a little warped he acted out his part completely; he claimed she had gotten away with eating both chicken legs at what he called the royal feast.

It put a chill in Leona when he started calling her those ugly names and pretending he could slap her was the last straw, Leona wasn't going to have that, Jerry had tried to run when he seen her getting angry.

Leona caught him and started hitting him knowing he wasn't allowed to hit her back, she started pounding on his face and chest, with the temper she had it would have been no telling how bad the boy would have been beaten if their mother hadn't came along when she did and took Leona off him.

The next day after school Jerry wouldn't talk to Leona, she had told all the kids at school what she had done and the boys really teased him, saying he was beat up by his sister and with the black eye he had he couldn't deny it.

They started calling him a little sissy because his sister wasn't as big as he was and she got the best of him, Jerry knew this harassment from the other kids wasn't going to go away anytime soon and swore to Leona he would never speak to her again.

The only thing Leona could do to make peace with her brother, was to give the only terms he would understand, telling him if he didn't start talking to her she would beat him up in front of his friends.

It didn't take Jerry very long to give her way to her and knew she would have done what she had said if he hadn't, the two of them continued to have sibling rivalry and it seemed to disappear the same way as it started.

Nether of them could remember why they were so mean to each other.

The years had past quickly and Leona was starting her freshman year in high school she had grown into a beautiful young lady everyone knew this except for her especially when she looked in the mirror.

Leona wasn't a happy camper she had brasses on her teeth and was very shy around the other students she tried avoiding talking to anyone if she didn't have to speak, it was like her hand had grown to her face the way she kept trying to cover her mouth with her hand. She just felt better keeping those brasses hid even though it seemed awkward to others when she spoke not removing her hand.

Sometimes people do have awkward characteristics some do meet in the most unusual ways that develops into a very special relationships, it seems these types of individuals have a lasting bond that grows stronger as years go by.

"Mystical Splendor" was the two words that came in the mind of a young teen age boy when he was asked how he would define love, there is always something special about young love, that first love that seems to enrage the parents of the teens.

The love two young teenagers share in all its awkwardness is something splendid to see especially if there someone else's children that are acting completely nauseating.

Daryl Moonie was just the kind of person who like the very thought of falling in love he got lots of practice thinking about how to go about it since he was too scared to even talk to girls.

It was in the fall of nineteen fifty two in Ellisville West Virginia, Where Daryl Moonie first laid eyes on Leona Martin, she was a freshman in high school and Daryl was a sophomore, it was something about the way her pony tail bounced when she walked that made him attracted to her.

For weeks he would always try to be in a location to see her walk into a class room sometimes he would be late for class because when he saw her he forgot that he was even in school.

Daryl's only thought was he would like to meet her and say hello and wondered if she would even speak to him, Daryl would hope that someone would at least bump into her.

Daryl figured if she dropped her books he would have a reason to approach her and he could say hello as he helped her pick up her books and he would get a chance to hear her voice as she said thank you.

Daryl's mom called him a late bloomer because his voice hadn't changed from being a child to being an adolescent, his voice would go from a low key voice to a high pitch and more times than not he would be the butt end of a lot of the kids jokes.

It seemed they really got a lot of laughs at his expense so he became very self conscious and tried to avoid speaking because he never knew what his voice was going to sound like.

Several times he would pass Leona in the hall way and wanted "so desperately!" to say something but was afraid if his voice squeaked he would ruin all chances of getting her to reply even to hello.

Daryl would carry a small bottle with a mixture inside containing lemon and honey; he was told it would keep his voice from cracking if he swallowed it right before he spoke.

In Daryl's mined he thought he knew how to overcome this if he could just get three or four words out it would be enough so he could hear her talk and he just knew her voice would be like music to his ears.

The only problem was all he could do was smile when she walked by, Daryl would practice at home looking in a mirror at his face and try to smile different ways to get her to say hello, all he wanted to hear from her was hi "I'm Leona Martin!".

Daryl had gotten so frustrated no matter how he smiled he couldn't get her to say a thing, football season was approaching and Daryl saw her in the gymnasium practicing with the other cheer leaders.

Daryl was quick to think on his feet, he snuck into the gym went under the bleachers and would sit under there day dreaming as he listened to Leona cheering.

Daryl had it bad this thing called puppy love he like everything she did in his mined she was doing it all just for him and knew if he could become a football player she would even notice him more and if he played his cards right he might even get her to look at him.

Awe the things this teen would think about while he was in his private little trance, he would envision himself out on the football field, he had just caught a pass, smiling he knew could run out of balance and possibly run into her.

In his vision he figured he could take his time apologizing to her and tell her how great a cheer leader she was then put her hand in his so all the other boys could see and show them how pretty she was.

Daryl believed the whole school would envy him if he should get hurt by being tackled knowing this girl took the time to see if he was alright and knew she would asked him if they could go steady.

Then quick as a flash he was bought out of his daydream hearing a voice say "hey you!", "come out from under there!", "what do you think you are doing!"

Not completely out of his daydream looked at the girls gym teacher and replied falling in love in a squeaky voice smiling as he heard the girls laugh.

Leona smiled as he continued to say he had a million things to share with the prettiest girl in school, the gym teacher told him to share them after school and told him to be on his way.

Daryl stood there for a moment returning to his daydreaming he envisioned her shouting his name as he made a touch down and heard her say "where did it go Daryl!", as he acted nonchalant and would look at her smiling and then wave, Daryl was coming out of his trance as the teacher was shoving him out the gym door telling him "to get to class".

Daryl gave it his all during football tryouts, he tried playing right tackle but got knocked around by the bigger boys, he then tried for the position of wide receiver but wasn't fast enough.

After trying all the other positions he went for quarter back but just couldn't remember the plays he was suppose to execute, no matter what position he tried he just couldn't make the grade.

Daryl knew he could stay on the team, but would probably never get a chance to play and knew he couldn't impress her by setting on the bench.

Daryl was running out of ideas and figured he would never get a chance to meet the girl that he fell head over heels in love with, until he woke up one morning and smelt bacon frying.

Daryl went downstairs to breakfast and heard his mom say well listen to that, no more squeaking, my son has finally matured as she winked at him saying what is it my young man wants for breakfast.

Daryl was so happy that when he went to school he marched right up to Leona Martin and said hello my name is Daryl Moonie and "I love you!" he couldn't believe what he had just uttered.

Daryl stood there with his mouth gapped open and saw her face turn red and she said, I'm Leona Martin and he said, "say it again!" and she said say what again, he said "your name!", "please tell me your name again!", you don't know how long I waited just for you to say what your name was, she said that's silly.

Right away Daryl figure he had better keep this conversation moving, Daryl said do you know what my favorite number is and she replied of course not "how could I!"

Daryl laughed saying I'm sorry its one hundred and thirty eight, that's how far it is from the tree to where a cluster of rocks are, its my secret place, when I marry you, I will take you there.

She looked at him briefly grinned saying that's nice and started laughing, without missing a beat she replied I wondered who my husband would be.

Then looking at him seriously commented she thought he should know she had wanted to speak to him for a long time too as tears started forming in her eyes, then started sniffling as she spoke.

Leona tried to explain to this moon eyed boy she was ashamed of her braces and he smiled saying let me see them and when she smiled he told her they were perfect.

Leona replied yea they are pretty cool huh, being in awe that she spoke to him Daryl seemed to be in a trance, saying he was sorry asking her what was it she had said, she answered asking him if he would you like to carry her books after school.

Daryl replied sure why not, saying he thought he would like that and she told him she would meet him out front after school, he answered her saying cool it's a date.

Daryl jumped straight into the air and saying we got a date and shouted down the hall way, Leona was embarrassed when she saw the other kids looking at her when Daryl kept saying he had a date with Leona Martin the pretties girl in the whole school and she replied "stop it you silly boy!" and go to your class before you are late.

He laughed saying anything you say my lady as he started running down the hall way jumping up and down calling out Leona spoke to me and we are going to be married.

Daryl and Leona were inseparable during high school becoming king and queen of their high school prom and their relationship extended into collage.

They would see each other as often as they could and sometimes that was difficult for them not being able to go to the same collage, however there love carried them trough the years.

Daryl worked his way through collage doing one odd job then another, until he finally earned his maters degree in chemistry and became a high school teacher.

He would teach a branch of science dealing with the structure, composition, properties, and reactive characteristics of substances, especially at the atomic and molecular levels.

Daryl thought it was important for students to know something that could make life easier on man, could also destroy him.

Daryl and Leona were married right after collage, Leona's last year in collage was disappointing to her she studied to be a doctor and was held back because of predigest in the school system.

In the fifties most of collage professors didn't think women could be or should be a doctor, Leona like this field and let several know how she felt her words fell on deaf ears.

Leona found herself swallowing her pride decided she would settle at being a RN and knew sometime in the future she would make her dream come true.

Daryl and Leona went on there honey moon in New Mexico, where Daryl studied Chemistry and Biochemistry at New Mexico State University.

He had told Leona so much about New Mexico she just had to go there and see this collage that made her husband so enthusiastic about teaching twelfth grade students.

The only thing Daryl loved more than teaching chemistry was the love he had for Leona; she was the air he breathed, the only beauty his eyes could see.

Daryl never lost the excitement he had for her, from the first day he saw her walk down the hallway of the very school where he is teaching.

He remembered every room she had a class in, memorized every cheer she had as a cheer leader, had a remembrance of the gleam that was in her eyes as they drank milk shakes at the malt shop.

Daryl especially remembered the day when she got her braces off and she couldn't wait to see what his kisses were like without them.

Daryl would smile when he characterized how the room would light up when she entered, Daryl tells everyone how she takes his breath away when she tells him that she loves him,.

He was overwhelmed by knowing he was the luckiest man in the world when he proposed to her and when he heard her utter the words I do, at their wedding.

People would laugh at the two of them when they were telling a story, how one would start talking and the other would finish a sentence.

Daryl and Leona after going on fourteen years of marriage still act as if they were on their honey moon they would embrace each other as if it had been there very first time both of them trembling with excitement always showing each other how much they mean to one another not so much in words but in their actions.

Daryl would come home after work peek in the window and look at his beautiful wife as she hurried with dinner knowing he would be there at any minute.

She wanted to have the meal on the table by six.

Leona would insist dinner should be promptly served at six pm, Daryl waited until the table was set and dinner was put on the table before he came into the house and would say he was sorry for being late asking her to forgive him.

He would tell Leona traffic was bumper to bumper, not knowing she always knew he was just outside the door never wanting to pressure her with anything.

Daryl would rather make up a story making out like it was his fault why dinner wasn't ready rather than to say a word to this woman who was the love of his life.

Leona found the rain was pouring down as she came running to her car, jumping in and then proceeded driving home after grocery shopping.

She was going to surprise Daryl and make his favorite meal Lasagna; Daryl wouldn't be home for another two hours and she could just see the look in his eyes when she took this dish out of the oven and hear him say food for kings topping it off with "alright lasagna!".

Then he would say thank you Leona my beautiful wife then sit and eat until he almost busted telling her she was the best cook in the world.

She could hear him say "what do you have for dessert" and knew what his response would be when she said cherry cheese cake.

She smiled to herself knowing he would go to the window and start shouting Leona is the greatest and wouldn't stop until one of the neighbors would say pipe down and it was usually from a neighbor four blocks down the street.

Leona stares at the clock while she is setting at the table knowing that Daryl would be home any minute she decided to take the lasagna out of the oven and set it on the top of the stove when she heard a knock at the door.

She called out I will be right there honey saying she had to sit the lasagna on the table asking him if he had forgotten his keys again.

When she went to the door it was one of Daryl's coworkers and he asked if Daryl was at home, Leona replied no but he should be there at any moment asking if there were something she could help him with and he replied no he was just enquiring why Daryl wasn't at school.

What the odd thing is he remarked Daryl's car is parked there, Leona told him he had left that morning to go to work and asked him if he was sure he wasn't at school and he answered saying he was certain of it.

He told her he had to teach one of his classes for him telling her when he saw his car was still there he thought maybe she had come and got him for some reason.

He told Leona he didn't think too much about it until after school was over and the students had all left, he noticed his car was in the parking lot and he commented Daryl always would run to his car so he would be the first to leave the school campus.

He asked Leona to call him and let him know if Daryl made it home alright, Leona smiled saying she was sure Daryl was fine and thanked him for coming by saying she would call him as soon as Daryl got there.

Watching the door close as Daryl's coworker left Leona started looking out the window then Leona started remembering what happened earlier that morning.

This was their anniversary marking it their fourteenth; she thought about Daryl getting up early to make breakfast for her and served it to her while she was in bed.

He had lit candles all over there room and placed a dozen roses on her night stand with a card saying happy anniversary my darling.

Daryl sat on the foot locker at the foot of their bed, waiting for her to open her eyes and hear her say good morning, Daryl wouldn't have cared if he was late for work, their anniversary was the most important day of his life.

He didn't mind setting and watching the most beautiful girl while she laid sleeping, knowing he was the luckiest man alive just to be in her presence made him fill like royalty.

He liked to watch her nose twitch knowing she was waking up from her dreams and he always wanted to be the first thing she would see of a morning.

He loved everything about her smile and was excited to hear her say good morning, he would set patiently while she was freshen up afterwards it seemed like she glided across the room when she came to him smothering him with her kisses.

Then she would jump back in bed so he could serve her breakfast, Leona had a way about her saying darling you'll be late for work and at the same time would want him to stay as she held on to him as long as possible before he had to leave the house.

The last words she heard him say was he loved her.

The same ritual he displayed everyday of their married life.

Always a kiss before he walked away saying he loved her and waited for her to reply saying she loved him too before he walked out the door.

Leona was worried; Daryl never in the fourteen years of marriage had ever been late coming home from work, she could set her watch by his promptness.

Leona found herself sitting in the middle of the floor looking at the door as time past by and hoping her only love would soon come through it.

Leona sat there in the darkness as it approached silently praying for the Lord to watch over him and keep him safe as she was fighting back tears as the feeling of emptiness came over her.

A chill had penetrated to the very core of her being and she sat there through the night then watched the sun come up as she watched the door and was saying to herself Daryl please come home.

Leona's hands were shaking when she picked up the phone and called the police after she had called all the hospitals and none of them had a patient by the name of Daryl Moonie.

It was eight thirty that morning when Leona made the call telling the police her husband was missing and told them about his coworker coming by and what he had told her. Everyone knew Leona and Daryl in their neighbor hood and knew Daryl wasn't the type of man who would just decide to get up one morning and leave without saying a word.

They would be some mornings they would see him set in his car just staring at the house and one of his neighbors asked him why he had done that.

Daryl would say he wanted to get a glimpse of his wife before he left that he hated going to work and leaving her alone.

The police questioned all the neighbors and the entire staff at the high school trying to figure out why Daryl would drive to school and leave his car not saying a word to anyone and would just disappear. The only response they had received from all the staff was Daryl wouldn't just disappear he loved his wife to much to leave without a word.

The police had Leona in tears after questioning her and suggested she knew what happened to her husband and started to interrogate her for several hours.

The police would make false accusations trying to get her to make a false statement that would make their job easier for them if they could lay the blame on her.

Going against her attorney's advice she consented to a polygraph test and then they let her leave the station but told her not to leave town. Leona felt like she had been violated after the crude way she had been questioned and all she wanted to do was go home and get in the shower.

She wanted to wash off of the stench of their words and wondered why anyone would talk to a person the way they did her, knowing if they had said something like that in the presence of her husband they would be eating their words. Leona commented saying she was a tax payer and help pay the police's salaries to protect her instead of that they were trying to persecute her.

One week has gone by and Leona still hasn't heard a word from the police, when she would call them some would give her a smart answer saying to her you tell us where he is or your guess is good as ours while others told her they were expanding their search.

Leona felt the only thing they were doing was ignoring the fact he was missing even though they said they were going to put out a bulletin across the United States.

The police knew it would be hard to find her husband with the crime rate that was over twenty thousand that year especially if her husband had been a victim of foul play.

They also knew they would find him eventually if he hadn't been buried in a sallow grave somewhere, four weeks has past as the detectives approached Leona's house.

One of the officers told her it had been confirmed that her husband's body had been found in Glendale, New Mexico lying in a parking lot in front of a high school.

They told her all the staff in the school had been questioned and no one there seemed to know her husband they assumed he had left Leona for another woman.

They called his murder a crime of passion.

Leona broke out screaming as the loss of her husband entered her thoughts telling the police they had to be mistaking that her husband had to be safe somewhere.

She refused to believe he was dead yet the pain she felt tore her completely apart and she woke up in the hospital after having a nervous break down.

Leona's family gathered around her trying to give her comfort and support but the only thing that would comfort her was for her husband to come back to her unharmed.

Leona's brother Jerry would go with her to New Mexico to bring his body back home she kept thinking to herself when she got there the man they claimed to be her husband wouldn't be in the morgue.

When the Mortician showed her the body, she fell on top of the man she loved so dearly and kept saying to him I can't live without you please wake up and then fainted.

When she woke she told Jerry while lying unconscious she was dreaming and she saw Daryl walk into their house he put his arms around her telling her he was alright.

He didn't understand why people wouldn't believe her and kissed her and she felt herself melting in his arms, saying I love you darling as she felt him starting to shake her.

Leona cried out "why are you doing this!" "I don't want you to go please stay with me Daryl!"

Jerry looked at his heart broken sister then told her that he was taking her to the motel and told her to wait at the motel until he could make arrangements for Daryl to be taken back to Ellisville. Jerry told her to try and get some rest.

Leona walked around in a daze from the sedatives the doctor had given her she couldn't determine one day from another.

It was like she was stuck in a time warp as she heard Jerry say Leona you got to snap out of this and saw him take her pills.

She heard Jerry saying you have taken all these you are going to pulling her to her feet and started walking her around the room forcing her to drink coffee.

Jerry became angry and started scolding her saying "come on Leona fight this!" you cant live in a dream world "he is gone!" and its time you started facing the fact "he isn't coming back!"

Leona screamed in anguish for the love of her life to return to her and felt her body wavering as Jerry walked her around the room and she collapsed as he held on to her.

Jerry picked her up carried her across the room laying her on her bed and apologized saying I'm sorry sis; saying he loved her then said rest now we will try again later.

Leona sleep through the rest of the day and woke the next morning smelling the aroma of coffee in the air as she stood and stumbled to the door.

Jerry saw her in the hall way as he went to her saying good morning and helped her to the table and poured her a cup of coffee.

Leona wasn't saying a word as she sipped on the coffee and then broke down into tears, Jerry walked over to her putting his arms around her telling her he would always be there for her.

Jerry told her to lean on him they would get through this together and he held her for hours as the tears keep flowing she released the last of the torment she was filling over the loss of her cell mate.

Leona felt like a part of her very being was gone leaving her filling empty inside not being able to say goodbye to the man whom she loved her with all her heart.

Ten days has past after they laid Daryl to rest.

Jerry made a daily routine of going to the cemetery picking his sister up off the grave of her husband while she begged him to let her stay.

Leona went from grieved stricken to being angry and wanted to know why the police hadn't caught the person who took the life of the only man she had ever loved.

As Daryl lay dieing he tried to tell who had killed him when he wrote the word "crimson" with his own blood and died as he was pulling his hand back from the word.

Daryl left a blood trail from the word to his fingertip, that had only moved a couple of inches away, Police was baffled on what this word meant and through all their efforts was drawing a blank of what it had to do with his murderer.

Trying to figure out why he came to this town in New Mexico would be a question that they would never get an answer to in their investigation.

Leona knew if the killer was ever going to be caught she would half to find a key to unlock the mystery behind this crime.

Solving this mystery laid in one word "crimson" and she knew in her heart there had to be someone, some where, that could solve this mystery.

Leona wasn't about to give up on finding her husbands murderer. Leona would cry herself to sleep at night after she had placed a reward in the news paper for anyone that could give any information on who might have seen her husband taken.

Leona wrote saying anything they could do to assist the police with their search and bring the guilty party to justice would be taken into consideration; hundreds of people called and most were willing to say anything in the hopes that she would give the reward to them.

Some would call just to threaten her saying she knew who the murderer was and she only done this to throw off the police in their investigation telling her she better watch her back.

Leona's didn't pay any attention to the simpletons' threats she knew they didn't know where she lived and had her phone number changed.

Leona knew she was a long way from being the perfect example of how a wife should act after her husband was murdered.

She hadn't realized their was a book one could read that told how to act if a spouse was killed, she told the public the same thing she had said to the police put their sources on finding the murderer.

The sad thing was her family would try to encourage her to stop this thing they called madness and to get on with her life.

They would say to her just to except Daryl's murderer got away and told her she needed stop wasting her only means of support by looking for a ghost before she went completely crazy.

Leona felt like pulling her out it wasn't because she believed the murderer had got away it was because of all the pessimists she had to endure.

Not once did Leona waver in her resolve to find the truth.

She told them Daryl was her life and she would spend the rest of her life trying to find those who may be responsible for taking him away from her.

Leona also told them if they couldn't be part of the solution; try not to be a part of the problem if they didn't want to help that was fine just quit trying to discourage her from finding out the truth.

Leona would call the police station often only to find out several months later that they had already closed the case file on her husband marking it as an unsolved murder.

They claimed they had no other choice after exploring all the avenues they had at their disposal they went through all the leads they had.

Leona felt so helpless and alone it seemed no one cared that he was killed except for her and that made her angrier yet and gave her the strength she needed to go after whoever the murder was.

Leona quest might seem ridicules to some finding out the truth and bring closure, she told people she would rather be dead than to give up on Daryl.

Leona knew he knew who had killed him and tried his best to tell who the murderer was and she wasn't going to rest until she had found out the reason why he was killed.

Leona found herself day dreaming a lot remembering the life she had with Daryl and she could almost hear him say Leona don't let this go away find them and she would start talking to him as if he were there.

All Leona could do was cry when she realized he wasn't.

For almost two years Leona would hire one detective after another and would act so brave when they told her they couldn't find a clue on how to solve the mystery behind Daryl's death.

Never once did she allow that to stop her in her pursuit to find the murderer.

Daryl's high school reunion would be held in two weeks the class of nineteen fifty four and Leona was determined to go there in the hopes that one of his buddies might have seen him at the school.

Hoping they just needed time to bring themselves to say something and if they did she was going to be there and hear everything they had to say.

But through the events of the evening not one came forward to say a word and Leona's hopes had been crushed sixty students graduated the same day as Daryl.

She was thinking there would have been at least one person that could tell her something, but found not to many of the people who attended the reunion even knew him and they felt awkward about her even being there and would avoid her as much as possible.

Draining herself complete, both mentally and physically Leona knew if she was ever going to find any answers, she had to start taking better care of herself.

Forcing her self to get up the next morning, Leona decided that she needed to get her mind fresh and quit thinking so much.

She was just beating herself up, by asking so many questions in her mind, that she couldn't find the answers to, she finally thought to herself sometimes you have to step back and look at the direction you needed to go in instead of pushing forward blindly.

Leona decided she would get away for awhile and started packing her suit case, not knowing where she was going or when she would return.

Jerry tried his best to get her to stay saying no matter where she went they couldn't find any more answers for her she told him she loved him but to "butt out!"

Leona told him as cheap as it was she didn't want his advise she emphasized that he didn't care enough to stick by her and support her as he promised he would now he didn't have to she was going.

She told him if she really believed the murderer couldn't be found her life would be over there would be no point of her living another second.

Leaving Ellisville would be the last thing that anyone would have ever thought Leona would do but those who were close to her thought they understood why she needed to get away.

Even though they felt guilty and was not about to admit it, her friends and family were glad she was leaving; they didn't think they could last another year of hearing about Daryl, they to needed to give it a rest.

It showed how little they really knew her she just needing a new perspective on how to look for the killer and not be in a place where everyone except her thought it was hopeless. Leona was heading out of town and she noticed a small park and saw there were lots of children there playing and thought to herself it would have been nice if she were able to have a child.

Daryl never mentioned it because he wouldn't say anything to her that he thought might upset her so the question about children never entered their conversations once he knew she wasn't able to have children.

Leona would have been willing to adopt but she figured if Daryl wanted to do that he would have suggested it and figured they had plenty of time to talk about a family.

Leona knew her savings were almost gone and knew she would half to go back to work being trained to be a doctor and only was allowed to be a registered nurse.

Leona was sure she could get a job about anywhere she wanted to go and decided to head west and completely change her life style, she stop at a restaurant somewhere in Georgia.

The life style they had seemed to be much like the one she was accustomed to and she knew she had made the right decision by going west.

Leona would drive from state to state stopping along the way to look at different towns and the people finding most of them were pretty much like everyone else.

She knew she needed a different pace and a completely different way of life she only hoped she could find a place that appealed to her.

She called her brother Jerry and asked him to sell her house and everything in it and told him she would let him know where to send the money.

She knew there was a big demand for homes in the area she lived and it shouldn't take to long before the house was sold.

Jerry tried to change her mind and told her when she realized there were no more answers to her finding Daryl's killer she would need her home.

Leona told him to forget it she would call a realtor to take care of it for her and told Jerry once again he was a disappointment to her saying three times is a charm.

Jerry was losing his sister and if he didn't start being a brother to her she would forget all of their childhood they shared together she needed his support not his grief.

Leona finally settled in a small town in Nebraska called Hastings she thought it was just the right place after all kool aid was invented there.

Once she had swallowed a glass of this refreshing drink she knew this place would be as good as any she had seen and decided to stay there.

Leona held true to her word she did change her life style from bad to worse acting like she had no reason to live until she met Fanny Mae Riggings "a neighborhood ding bat".

This woman made it a point to let all new comers know who she was and would always stick her nose in where it didn't belong.

It didn't take her long to figure out Leona was starting to be unstable and one thing Fanny couldn't stand was a person to fill sorry for themselves.

Fanny told Leona if she wanted to die she would kill her and if she didn't straighten up she wouldn't have to ask her to do it.

Leona looked at this woman and started laughing she thought she was hilarious the way her eyes bulged when she talked and loved the way she just came right out and said what was on her mind.

This was going to be the start of a good friendship and Leona was thankful she had come along when she did a new place a new friend was what this doctor ordered.

Pushing forty Leona was still a vision of beauty and several of the men there had stated that fact to her while they were pursuing an opportunity to get to know her better.

They soon found out in a hurry she wasn't interested even though she thought it was still nice to hear someone thought she was still attractive.

For over a year Leona wrapped herself up in work pulling double shifts filling in for anyone that needing her to trying to keep her mind off the very thing that has been bothering her. Leona thought often of her love she had for her brother and didn't like the fact that he hadn't made an attempt to talk to her and was filling very hurt over it.

He had always given in to her only time would tell if he was going to be the brother she knew he could be, Leona was thinking why isn't he here where I need him most.

Leona loved to talk about Daryl and that was why she liked Fanny so much she could talk about him for hours and Fanny liked hearing her talk about him.

She told Leona her life was better than a soap opera and never wanted Leona to end the story, Leona was trying to save money in order to pursue her quest.

She promised herself she would find out who was responsible for Daryl's death and knew it would cost thousands hiring private investigators.

She spent most all her savings after paying the investigators who never found any clues and on a nurses salary wasn't enough to pay any investigator for a very long period.

After her house was sold and the ten year mortgage that was left had been paid, Leona still had enough to buy herself a used mobile home already set up on a piece of land.

She was thankful she didn't half to pay rent, even though this abode she had to live in wasn't what she had been accustomed to.

Jerry finally called her and tried to make peace telling her he was coming to visit her he stayed with her for nearly three months.

She wouldn't except money from him when he offered and hugged him saying all she needed from him was his love, so he fixed her mobile home and made her place a very nice little home.

But Jerry made one big mistake he bought a friend for her to meet, Leona and Fanny were playing gin when they arrived and Leona sent the both of them packing.

Leona wasn't very happy with her brother and let him know so in no uncertain terms, Jerry screamed at her to go on with her life and forget Daryl.

Jerry told her she was killing herself over a memory and begged her to let go but Leona was domineering and said she would never give up.

She told Jerry that Daryl couldn't rest until she found his murderer and told Jerry to go home and leave her alone Fanny told her to kick his back side.

She smilingly commented for Leona to let her do it she said the nerve of him getting someone for Leona and not even thinking about her.

Fanny looked at Leona and remarked Jerry was right about one thing Fanny told her she can't walk among the dead and find the living.

Fanny told her not to let anyone determine for her when she was ready to start another life with someone else.

Leona looked at her and told Fanny just to go home she had heard more than enough for one evening and Fanny replied she didn't have to knock her over with hints saying she would just go.

She kissed Leona on the cheek on her way out the door looking at Jerry told him to do as his sister asked or he would answer to her saying "now go!"

Jerry knew Fanny was a little loony and she would shoot someone in a heart beat if they got on her wrong side.

He didn't say a word he went into the bedroom to get his things as he was leaving he told Leona to call if she ever needed him.

Two months had passed Leona's dad had gotten very ill and wanted to see Leona and asked for her to come back to Ellisville to visit him.

She returned to Ellisville and stayed with her mom and dad for almost a month until her dad died she loved her dad as much as she did Daryl.

Leona never grieved the way she did over Daryl knowing it was old age and a bad heart that took him; even though she would miss him she was able to put closure to him.

This was something she wasn't able to do with Daryl.

Her dad left her a considerable sum of money and it was his wish that she spend it to help find Daryl's killer and in the note he left her he told her to be careful who she hired.

Her dad said he loved Daryl to for the simple fact he made her so happy a feat only a few women could enjoy and he told his daughter it was a privilege for him to know her husband.

He asked for her to start a new life with some one saying no one was meant to be a lone not even her, he told her to look in on her mother from time to time and see that Jerry did to. Leona knew her dad liked

her husband but never would have dreamed he wanted the same thing she did and knew he was right she didn't want to be alone.
 Under the circumstances she felt she didn't have any other choice.
 The life she had with Daryl was still a part of her and she wouldn't consider starting a new life until she could find closure to the one she had with Daryl.
Leona was thankful for her employers who allowed her to stay as long as she needed to be with her dad and they welcomed her back with open arms when she returned to work.
 All of her coworkers noticed a change in her they couldn't quite put their finger on a part of Leona no one had seen was starting to return.
 She wasn't as tense as she used to be and would even laugh when someone said something funny something none of her co workers had ever seen.
 With the money she managed to save and what was left to her by her father she knew she could get back on track and engage in her quest.
 Having the experience she had with private detectives she knew she could sort out the ones who were just looking to make a quick dollar.
 Leona hoped she would find someone who would put all his resources in finding the truth of her husband's death and allow her to continue with her life.
 Time was ticking away years and she hoped she once again could find happiness one she could share with someone for the remainder of her life.
This would be the year full of surprises to Leona it seemed all her friends in Ellisville had wanted to be apart of her quest.
 The letter that was sent to her by one of Daryl's and her friends said he had found an investigator whom he thought might figure out exactly what happened to Daryl.
If he were wrong they would at least help with the cost and he sent twenty five thousand dollars that he and some other of Daryl's friends had put together in order to help her with her quest.
Her friends finally was telling her they were sorry for not sticking by her they said they hoped she could forgive them and told her the money wasn't for them to try to clear their conscious.

They told Leona they hoped it would help and told her if she didn't want the money just to give it to charity saying to her not to give up as they had.

When Leona finished reading the letter she broke down in tears, she no longer felt she had to go it alone, she had people who cared and to her that was enough.

Leona thought Richard B. Beakers was an odd name, but thought to herself it wouldn't hurt to contact him and see what he could offer. Leona called his office in Chicago.

His secretary took a message after telling Leona to let her know how Mr. Beakers could be a service to her, Leona gave her all the details she could on the case and the secretary told her if Mr. Beaker thought he could help her he would notify her.

She also stated if he didn't contact her meant he wasn't interested in the case and Leona said what you mean he wouldn't be interested in the case.

She told Leona he only took cases if they were interesting to him, but assured her this might be one he might accept or she would have already told her he wouldn't be interested.

Nearly three years has passed since Daryl was killed and Leona knew it would be hard to find anyone who would take the case, especially the ones who really wanted to solve it.

Leona had no idea that Richard Beakers had chosen to take her case, he found it somewhat exhilarating, it had been a long time since he saw a case that he found challenging to him.

Richard had a contact at the police department in Ellisville, who allowed him to have a look at Daryl's case file and it seemed to him they had been quite thorough in their investigation.

But Richard never did go by anyone else's investigation, so he had a lot of foot work to do and he put his entire staff on this case and put all the rest of his cases on hold.

Richard said he would give it a few days to see how much he could find out then determine how many of his staff members he would need on this case.

Like the police Richard would start with Daryl's family and friends first, but he was a lot more discreet than the police and he thought to himself if he were going to find Daryl's killer he would have to become like Daryl and trace all his foot steps that lead him to the very person, who wanted to kill him, he would start by going to the school.

Posing as Mike Thurmond a High school chemistry teacher, he went to the High school were Daryl taught chemistry and applied for a temporary position.

Richard told them he wanted to give it a try before he committed himself to a full time position they told him they had a position open after one of their teachers had been killed.

He asked who the teacher was and they said Daryl Moonie they said they had several substitute teachers none of whom felt like they wanted to stay.

After they heard of Daryl's death, they must have thought someone might have something against chemistry teachers and was afraid they might be a target.

The school board assured Richard that was pure nonsense, Richard just laughed and replied time will tell asking if he were killed if they would say the same thing to the next teacher.

Richard gave impeccable credentials in this field and was hired on the spot, he knew Daryl was full of energy and displayed excitement in the class room and students had remarked how much he was like Daryl in that aspect.

Teachers were drawn in by his charm and seemed to confide in him every detail of their life and invited him to their homes and had him included in their car pools.

Richard was living the life of Daryl Moonie and after several months of this, Richard had cleared everyone from being a suspect, he went to the school board and resigned telling them he had a better offer.

Richard obtained a teaching position that was offered in New Mexico at the New Mexico State University in the Chemistry and Biochemistry department where he became a professor and taught the class.

He walked the hallways of the place where Daryl had got his Masters degree and would check on the odd jobs of Daryl's he knew about having them covered by his staff where Daryl had worked.

Richard wanted to find out everything he could about Daryl's life.

Richard knew the answer had to be here and was determined to find out how his collage years got him killed, Richard befriended all of the teachers that taught Daryl.

Richard found out he was well liked by all of them and over a period of time occasionally bringing up the subject in reference to Daryl.

They told him of Daryl's dedication and enthusiasm he had for learning, he was given "the Academy Gold Medal of Honor" for distinguished contribution to the advancement of Tran disciplinary Foundational ideas and activities.

They said he was offered a job as a professor in their university because of being in the top five of his class, but he turned them down and said he only wanted to teach high school students.

Richard was very impressed with Daryl's credentials and knew this would be one case he would solve or he would give up the detective agency.

Daryl reached for the stars and grasped them with both hands and put them in his pocket, never looking back to see what might have been, just made his dreams a reality.

Daryl gave his all to everything that meant something to him and earned respect from everyone that knew him, Richard became very found of this man.

Richard remarked to his associates he had never met this man but would have enjoyed his company, because he knew that they could have been friends.

Richard was working with a chemist whom he hired to tutor him while he was acting the part of a professor having him to set up all the class projects.

Using a transmitter for him to let him know exactly how to perform any task he was going to do and the chemist was monitoring his movements from a closet in the class room. This would keep his cover, so he could continue working as a professor; the chemist was a class mate of Richard's dad in collage and had gotten Richard an interview for the position at the collage.

When Richard told him about the case he was working on and the professor was more than glad to help him anyway he could.

Richard was on the job for over six months had entertained everyone that associated with Daryl and now was in the process of elimination.

Him and his staff work at interviewing all the people he worked with at his part time jobs and he suspected one of them had killed Daryl. Richard didn't know what the motive was and so far none of them had one Richard had eliminated the teachers and professors of the collage and was sure it was one of his class mates.

After giving this theory much thought Richard had several of his staff following up on his theory they worked long hours, eliminating one person than another.

Richard decided to leave the University after running into a dead end with the staff and go and meet Daryl's wife convinced she had nothing to do with his murder.

However Richard wanted to see for himself what kind of woman Daryl had chose to spend the rest of his life with and knew she had to be an extraordinary woman for him to even give her a second glance? Richard chose to put her under surveillance not as a suspect, but as a creature of curiosity a job he felt some what reluctant in doing.

He wanted to see for himself why this woman had a drive to find the person responsible for her husband's death, because most women would have went on with their lives after the police had done their investigation.

No matter how it turned out for Richard that was impressive in its self after seeing this woman Richard thought her beauty would take any mans breath away.

The poise she showed in the way she walked, the way her hair bounced, he found himself being very attracted to her, he knew he couldn't continue this surveillance.

After following her around for over a week, he felt like a peeping Tom and it discussed him that he allowed himself to go as far as he did.

Fifteen months had past since Leona called his office and Richard had to let her know what he had been up to and hoped she understand his motives.

Richard hoped she wouldn't be angry with him for not contacting her sooner but he knew weather she was or not wouldn't matter he was set on finding Daryl's killer.

He made an attempt to meet her by calling her home getting her answering service Richard left her a message and told her he would like to meet with her.

Richard asked her to come to the motel where he was staying that he would meet her in the lobby and they could go somewhere for coffee and have a chat.

Leona was somewhat puzzled over the message he left and decided to take a friend with her as he interviewed her being hesitant Leona not really wanting to meet him.

Leona figured by taking someone along he might not even show his face when she and her friend entered the lobby of the motel.

Leona went to the front desk and had them to page him as he walked toward her and her friend Leona felt like somehow she knew him as she spoke to him saying hello.

She looked as Richard and said I'm Leona and asked him if they had ever met and he replied to her saying no we haven't and she commented that it was odd she felt for sure she had seen him some where.

She told him she never forgot a face and she told him it would come to her where it was she had seen him Richard was baffled why she thought she had ever seen him.

Richard thought to himself that he must have one of those faces people like to think they recognize there was a small coffee shop within walking distance of the motel.

Leona told her friend on the way out of the motel that she could leave and her friend said alright if that's what you want but are you going to be alright.

Leona replied of course she would be that he watched her home for over a week and never tried to harm her, so she figure he was safe, saying go ahead that she would be fine.

Richard didn't know what to say for the first time in his life he was speechless he had never been on surveillance that the person he was watching had seen him and knew this woman was exceptional.

When her friend left she told Richard she was caring mace and if he tried anything she knew how to use it and asked him now what was it he wanted to talk to her about.

Before he could answer her, she stated she knew he had been watching her that's why she had a friend watching him and knew he was telling the truth.

Richard asked what truth Leona replied when you said you were staying at this motel silly, when she saw his face she knew exactly who he was and he laughingly replied do you want a job.

She smiled saying no thanks she has one not seeing why he was amused told him he already knew that to, she told him she saw him in the parking lot several times at the hospital. Leona asked him if he wanted her to give him, his tag number and started to open her purse, she told him his secretary's name was Sheryl.

Leona continued to say his secretary is the mother of two children, her husband is a police officer and you became a private eye after you left the police department in New York.

Leona told him he was married for two years his wife's name was Blanch she had been cheating on you and you broke her lovers jaw.

Leona told him he was suspended from his job because of it and he got so angry he quit the police force and that's when he became a private investigator.

At first she remarked he would only except those kinds of cases until he had enough of being someone else's peeping tom and then he started taking on cases that fit his own profile of being a detective.

A field you were very good at she confirming his credentials do you want to hear more Leona asked handing him the tag number to his car.

She commented she thought about what his secretary had said and asked him what he was doing there after all this time.

She told him she didn't figure Daryl's murder was challenging enough for him and didn't think he was interested.

He looked directly in her eyes saying he saw that she had done her home work she replied yes she had and told him she was not sure he could help her.

Leona started to get up from the chair at the table where they were seated Richard asked for her to stay for a few minutes asking her did she know he had been working on her husband's case for over a year and never approached her or even asked her for a dime.

Richard asked her if she would give him the courtesy to speak saying he would like for her to sit back down saying we have more to discuss that's if she was really interested in finding out who killed your husband.

Richard told her he did not like to toot his own horn however he was going to he told her he was the very best at what he did.

He told her he never charged anyone until he had solved their case.

Richard told her they pay him only if he allowed them to pay in her case he suggested he would like for her to go with him to Chicago and help him sort out all he had found that she knew better than anyone the movements of her husband.

He told Leona it seems she had a real good eye for seeing the truth and told her he needed someone that is willing to work on this case pro bono.

Is that right Leona replied saying she saw the way he looked at her asking him if he thought he was Gods gift to women saying he only wanted her to go with him to see how far he can take a grieving widow.

Richard replied he was sorry she felt that way he thought they could work together telling her he was sorry he bothered her and got up from the table and walked out of the coffee shop.

Leona didn't know what to think, he was right she didn't know he had been working all this time on Daryl's case and said to herself she would give him the benefit of doubt.

Leona went running out of the coffee shop called out to him, saying she would get a leave of absence from her job, saying they could leave at the end of the week that is if he still wanted her to go with him.

Richard turned and looked at her asking her if she was sure this is what she wanted to do seeing her smile he answered her by saying that's fine and asked her if she would have lunch with him.

Richard told her she could pay for that, although she thought it was odd he asked her out for dinner, she replied sure why not.

Leona told him they would go get her car at the motel and looked him in his eyes and thanked him for all he had done so far and told him she would write him a check for what he had already done.

Richard smiled saying he didn't think she had that kind of money to pay for a case that hasn't gotten anywhere yet saying lets just see how it goes and then we will decide how much you should pay.

She replied he had better tell her soon, she might not be able to afford him he laughed saying me probably you could afford then told her his staff he couldn't even afford so forget about it for now.

Richard told her they a lot of work to do.

Leona asked him if he liked Italian food he said yes that it was alright but confessed he was more of a meat and potato kind of guy.

Leona smiled saying finally a man who knows what he likes and is sticking to his guns and he asked her what would she like and she replied her husband's killers head on a platter would suffice.

Richard squinted his eyes saying well lets see if we can't get him or her to stand trail and we will let a jury decide their fait the way justice is supposed to be served.

Leona was thinking to herself that it would be nice if he could fine if her husbands murderer only he wouldn't have the chance to go to trail.

Leona was thinking to herself she would give him as much as a chance as he had given her husband it didn't matter to her if she was executed for killing him.

At least she thought she would be with Daryl if there is any justice and that was all that mattered to her no matter what the investigator thought.

When they had finished eating Leona order a slice of cherry cheese cake and asked him if he would like some and he answered saying no thanks a piece of that blue berry pie with a scoop of vanilla ice cream would suite him just fine.

Leona smiled and asked the waiter to get it for him saying this poor man eats as if he were starved to death, Richard smiled saying he always did on someone else's dime.

The hour had passed quickly and Leona thought to herself how nice it was to have someone to eat with and have a conversation.

It had been a long time for her and she didn't want the lunch to end, finding herself attracted to a man she had only met a little over an hour ago.

She just figured the attraction was because she missed Daryl so much and he seemed interested in finding Daryl's killer or he wouldn't had spent so much time on it already. Leona figured it didn't hurt that he was handsome and knew he thought she was pretty to, by the quick glances he gave her, thinking she didn't notice.

Leona was thinking he was a little arrogant and with the reputation she heard he had, she figured he might deserve to be.

The next morning Leona saw a car sitting in her drive way and saw it was Richard, she stuck her head out the door and asked him to give her a few more minutes and he saw her start to put some luggage out on the porch.

Richard got out of the car and went to get her suit cases and told her not to carry them, he would get them for her and she smiled and remarked what a gentleman.

Richard made a smart comment saying not really he just want to get on the road and told her she needed to get it in gear.

Anger came over Leon's face as she was saying fine taking the luggage from his hands and almost falling as she went down the steps.

Richard caught her saying she was a typical woman getting angry over nothing picked up the bags and put them in his car and looked at her saying he did apologies for his behavior.

She told him she did understand saying she had made him wait almost an hour telling him it was no wonder he was getting upset but it wouldn't have bothered Daryl.

Leona started to cry as he went to her saying he was so sorry telling her it wouldn't happen again, then helped her into the car.

They had been traveling for hours neither one of them saying a word when Richard pulled over in a small filling station that had a picnic area; he asked her if she needed to stretch her legs that he really needed to, the part of stretching their legs sounded good to her.

They both went inside to freshen up and she walked back to the car handing him a cup of coffee and asked him if he wanted her to drive awhile.

Richard was stretching his arms and responded to her saying that sounds great that he could use a break she got under the steering wheel and started to go back on the interstate.

The silence had broken with the two of them as they talked about one thing and another Richard started singing Leona thought maybe it was something only he might enjoy so she thought she would help him out, as she started turning up the radio.

Richard started laughing at Leona knowing what she thought of his singing.

Richard had to fight himself not wanting her to know how hard it was for him not to look at her and had to force himself to look at the road instead.

Leona did notice and it sort of pleased her to know she still could turn a head in her direction and it gave her more of an opportunity to look at him.

She would smile when he would take a quick peek at her and said to herself just keep it under control Richard that's not why we are traveling together.

This fourteen hundred mile trip took them three days and it hadn't been long enough for either one of them, however neither one of them admitted to their attraction to one another.

When they started working on solving the death of her husband their mind set was strictly business, Leona started looking through some paper work and ran across some pictures.

These were some she had never seen before they were of Daryl lying in the parking lot of the school and she saw his hand lying under the word Crimson.

Leona eyes became blurry after the tears stated to flow down her checks, Richard had been out getting some reports from the wire service and when he returned he found Leona sitting in the middle of the floor.

Leona didn't hear Richard come in as she flipped through the pictures crying and saying Daryl please tell me who done this to you. Richard took off his jacket throwing it over the pictures helped Leona to her feet, setting her on the sofa and told her she wasn't suppose to have seen the pictures.

He apologized for them being among the papers she had been asked to go through, he didn't know the pictures were part of the papers he had given to her to go over.

Richard was looking through the reports he had received from some of his staff and slammed down on the table with his fist saying who are you.

Richard then told Leona he had been through every friend her husband had saying he couldn't find as much as a parking ticket saying how can anyone be as clean as his friends seem to be.

This doesn't make since one of his friends had to have killed him everything inside him points in that direction, Leona told Richard she had to go back to her motel.

Leona was tired and had enough for one day saying maybe tomorrow they would see something they have over looked, in the mean time she suggested he get some rest to.

Richard went to Leona's motel room the next morning to pick her up but she had already left, he thought he would take her out to get breakfast.

Richard was disappointed he had missed her and decided he would go alone he knew once he started on the paper work he would get so involved that he would forget to eat.

He hoped Leona had went for breakfast to but when he reached his office he had seen she had went back there and spent the night going through the paper work.

Leona was looking at more pictures of the school where Daryl was killed and asked Richard to look at the way her husband was laying on the pavement.

Richard looked saying what do you see Leona and she replied she wasn't sure but if he was killed there why is his body laying like it had been placed on the ground it didn't seem he could have fell like that she remarked.

Leona told him to look at the autopsy reports and Richard reluctantly asked what are you getting at Leona and she replied there is no bump on his head and Richard looked at his head not knowing where she was going with this asked her why there should be one.

Leona commented from what she had read in the report he was shot at a close range and more than likely the bullet would have picked him off his feet and he would plunged to the ground full force.

Leona remarked how could he not have a bump on his head when Richard took a closer look he replied that's a good question and he told her he would have one of the staff go to the morgue and ask one of the staff there if they could have been a bump on his head.

If you theory is right he replied we might be able to search the cars and see if we can find any traces of blood or fiber, although Richard was just trying to encourage her he didn't think there was anything unusual about the bodies position. It did make him slightly wonder if what she commented on might be what happened even though he felt like it was unlikely told her he knew she might see something none of them would have.

Richard smiled saying are you hungry lets go get some breakfast he turned to look at her when he hadn't heard a response but seen she was asleep setting on the sofa and he went to the closet to get a blanket.

He had stayed there several times himself.

Placing the blanket over her Richard whispered sleep beautiful lady as he returned to look through more of the pictures.

Richard stopped what he was doing and made several phone calls and went back to looking at the papers.

Richard had piled up stacks of papers on his desk two hours later hearing the phone ring answered it was one of his staff members.

He told Richard that the medical doctor that done the autopsy commented it was very possible he could have had bump on his head but in all probability he wouldn't.

He told him it wasn't in their report saying when he fell he would have landed on his back and his head might not have hit hard enough to cause a bump and if it had he would have most likely been unconscious.

His staff member told Richard to think about it saying he wouldn't have been able to spell the word "crimson" with his finger tip.

The doctor reported there was nothing about the way his body laid to indicate he was shot somewhere else and he managed to live long to be put in the parking lot of the school and spell out a word in blood.

It was three in the afternoon when Leona woke up, she got up stretching after sleeping so long in that awkward position and stumbled over to the desk and sat down wondering where everyone had went to.

Leona wrote a note to Richard telling him she went to the Motel to get a shower and for him to meet her in the lobby they could have dinner together if he liked.

Leona then raised up from the desk as she saw the report Richard had written that was marked was he or wasn't he moved, with a question mark attached.

Leona didn't think to much of it and then proceeded to her motel she felt like someone was following her and figured it was just her imagination.

Richard returned to his office at 4:30 pm and saw Leona's note and looked at his watch and thought to himself that he would join her for dinner.

Richard left for his home to get changed, Leona wanted to be prompt and hurried changing her clothes a dozen times and only took twenty minutes deciding what shoes she wanted to wear.

Leona smiled when she was completely dressed until she took a look at herself in the mirror it was hurry up and get change time again.

Leona was just putting on her shoes when she heard the knock on the door and she called out saying she would be right out.

When she opened the door she found a note lying on the floor she assumed it was from Richard telling her to meet him at the restaurant.

Boy did she ever get angry saying the nerve of him not coming to pick her up talking to herself commenced ranting saying she slaved to get the right dress and right shoes to wear.

"Now he is asking me to meet him!", then she started smiling when she thought sounded like a school girl looking down the hall way she saw a face that seemed to be familiar as a man had got on the elevator, Leona thought if he couldn't pick her up it was alright, thinking she would call him.

Leona was first wondering why he didn't just call her instead of sending her a note when Leona called Richard was on his way out the door and ran to answer the phone.

When she told him she didn't really want to go by herself to the restaurant he asked her what she was talking about and she looked confused saying the note you sent asking me to meet you there asking him if he had her rooms phone number saying you could have called.

Richard responded saying are you awake, she replied of course she was saying why did he ask such a silly thing he told her he didn't send a note telling her to wait there until he got to her.

Richard hung up the phone, when he arrived at the motel he went straight to her room he knocked on the door and when she opened it he whispered in her ear and told her to be quite.

Taking a debugging devise out of his briefcase, started going all over her room with it and told her it was alright telling her she could talk telling her they needed to leave the motel.

Richard suggest that he send for her things.

Richard told her he didn't know how but they had got close to her husband's killer now he may be trying to eliminate her Leona replied that's the way break it to me gently.

It may be nothing she told Richard but saw a man getting on the elevator who did look familiar telling Richard she couldn't think where she saw him before.

Richard asked her where the note was she went to the dresser picked up he note and handed it to him he started to read the note then told her from now on she had to be real careful.

He told Leona unless she saw his face, not to trust his voice if he said who he was without showing himself for her not to let him in.

She was not to go anywhere without him saying if you get any sudden visits from friends don't let them near you even if one of your family is with them don't let them in your door. Richard told her who ever they were dealing with was probably desperate and scared so it's no telling what he will do.

When they got to the restaurant Richard called his staff and told them to check for bugs in his office and to find out if anyone from Ellisville had flown to Chicago in the last month.

He said he wanted a report on his desk no later than noon the next day Leona asked him if it were possible the killer could be in the restaurant.

Richard said only if he is a mind reader he told her he made reservations at the Italian restaurant that she wanted to go to the one she left in her note for him.

Richard told her it's a good thing he is a meat and potato guy telling her he didn't need a reservation at this restaurant and smiled.

Richard told her he would have a man taking pictures of everyone in the Italian restaurant but he doubted if he is inside.

You never know, maybe we will get lucky.

Richard ordered for Leona to be watched twenty four seven and she was never to be left alone from that day forward if she needed an escort he would be the only one that had that privilege.

Leona knew Richard was attracted to her and felt guilty he hadn't charged her anything for working on Daryl's case and when they went to the office the next day, she asked him how he could pay all his staff to work on this case and she hadn't give him any money for his services.

He told her he had a similar case years ago a woman had lost her husband he was found dead only they thought he committed suicide.

She hired him to prove he was indeed murdered when the case was over and the killer was caught she gave him an ignoramus amount of money and told him to use it on cases the police couldn't solve.

Leona thought he was just feeding her a line and told him so. Richard took a letter out of a file showing her the woman's instructions and the amount of money she had given him

Leona told Richard she was sorry for doubting him.

They were going through the pictures that were sent to Richard, from the Italian restaurant, after carefully viewing each picture; Leona said she didn't know any of the people in the pictures.

However Richard said there were three bugs found in his office, who ever put them there was an amateur they even were able to lift a partial finger print from one of the bugs.

The reports indicated there was not one of Leona's or Daryl's friends who left Ellisville and came to Chicago in the last month.

Richard asked her if anyone of there friends moved away and she replied she was unaware of any of them leaving Ellisville.

Richard told Leona he wanted her to move back to Ellisville the murderer would only think two ways about this either he would come after her or figured she given up on the search and he would go on with his life.

Leona asked Richard if he was thinking about quitting the case and Richard told her if he decided to do that, he would also give up his detective agency saying lets see how your move will unfold first and told her not to worry.

Richard jokingly suggested the killer could only kill her once and told her to look on the bright side; he would be caught then smiled as turned around in his seat.

Leona didn't think it was funny nor did she like the sound of that murderer getting her before she could get him regardless how it would turn out she knew some how some day they would find him if it meant her death then so be it.

Leona told Richard she would do as he asked, Leona called her brother Jerry and told him she was coming home, she had decided to give up on the search and just wanted to go on with her life.

She told him she hadn't got a bit closer to finding the truth and asked him to pick her up at the airport the next morning and told Jerry her flight would be landing at eight o'clock am. When she hung the phone up she looked at Richard and asked why he wanted her to tell him that Richard replied his phone could have been easier to bug than his.

Richard told her he was certain the murder knows what she had told Jerry and he figured the killer would be watching her to see what her intensions were.

Richard had two of his staff members that were already on the plane and three more were at the airport just to watch her get on the plane.

There would be two more would be at the airport when she arrived home he told her she would be under constant watch.

He told her they would be men that would be on surveillance at her brothers and mothers home and told her not to worry

If he came after her his men would get him and told her she didn't need to pack her luggage it was being taken to the air port and he would be in touch.

Richard drove her to the air port and watched as she went inside, it was only a matter of minutes that Leona had boarded the plane and was in the air on her way back to Ellisville.

Leona hadn't had much rest on the plane and was exhausted when she walked into the airport; Jerry was waiting on her and called to her.

Leona was glad to see him and asked about their mother and he told her she was fine and was expecting them for dinner.

Leona told him that sounded good to her and told him she needed to get some rest Jerry winked saying he would have her at his house in no time saying then she could get some sleep.

When they arrived at Jerry's house, Leona looked around to see if see could she a car that might be watching them and she spotted two and knew one of them was the killer.

When they got inside Jerry asked her what she was looking at Leona and she replied nothing really she smiled saying it was just good to be back saying she always liked the neighbor hood he lived in.

She claimed she was looking to see if it had changed any since she was there last saying as far as she could tell nothing has and told him that was a good thing a nice neighborhood like he lived in should be a safe place to live.

She told Jerry they would talk later; she was going to lie down, Leona would have tried to contact Richard but knew Jerry's home was probably bugged and she would just half to wait on him to contact her.

Leona woke up late that afternoon and saw Jerry in the back yard, she walk out to see what he was doing and picked up a football saying catch throwing it at him.

Jerry looked at her asking her what she was doing out of bed saying he figured she would have slept a couple more hours and she replied she just couldn't wait to hear about his love life.

Leona enjoyed picking on her brother especially about his dating he sort of hesitant of saying anything knowing how intense his sister could be he smiled saying he could take her, their mom and the dog with him on any date that he had lately.

Giving a smirk like grin she told him she really believe that, saying you're a liar and he just laughed at her, she asked him when he was ever going to settle down and he replied I have sis I can't find anyone who will have me.

What you see is what I am, a free available bachelor, Leona picked up the water hose and started spraying him saying she would break him lying to her.

Jerry ran toward her to take the hose from her and spray her with it both of them laughing while each was struggling to spray the other. Leona was acting like her old self.

Jerry noticed this right away and the rest of the afternoon past quickly as they were inside getting dressed to go to their mothers' house and they were acting like clowns on the front lawn.

Both of them were arguing who was going to drive and Leona always got her way with her brother and smiled at him as she was backing out of the drive way.

Leona saw both cars were still watching the house.

Leona's mother was waiting on the front porch when they arrived and got up from the swing to greet her daughter she hadn't seen in over a year.

She hugged her when she walked up the steps and Leona noticed a car across the street and as she was walking in the house saw another had pulled in down the block and turned off his head lights.

No one got out of the car.

Jerry was up to his usual self, arguing with Leona for taking both of the chicken legs, while there mother was smiling at the two of them and told Jerry to leave his sister alone, as she did so often when they were children.

Leona was glad to be home and it was good for her to see her mother smile, it seemed they had just got there, when Jerry asked her if she was ready to go and she said not really and told her mother she would come by and visit her real soon.

As they were walking out the door Jerry ran to the car and got under the steering wheel as Leona dangled the car keys in her hand telling him to move over and Jerry slide across the seat of the car and Leona got under the steering wheel and backed out of the drive way.

Then Leona saw a glimpse of a man that slide down in his seat as she drove by and saw the head lights come on as she turned the corner.

\She wanted desperately to tell Jerry but knew if he acted strange; the murder might come after them both when they got to the house and went inside she told Jerry she wanted him to drop her off at her mothers house before he went to work telling him she seemed so happy to see them both together

Leona told him she wanted to get her out of the house and take her shopping telling him they would come by his job and they will have lunch together.

Jerry replied well here it goes again the family get together and she hit him on his shoulder and said you know you love it brother as she went into her bed room opened the window and jumped to the ground.

Leona wanted to see if she could spot anyone else besides the car across the street she was peeking around the corner when she felt a hand being put over her mouth and a voice saying what do you think your doing.

As the hand left her mouth, she saw it was Richard and told him she almost peed herself saying he scared the tar out of her.

He replied if it were the murder you wouldn't have had the chance to be scared and she told him what she saw and he answered her saying your to nose, that was me and helped her to get back through the window.

Richard didn't tell her he saw the same thing she did he wanting her to calm down and quit making stupid mistakes, like she just had and only hope they weren't seen.

Just as Richard walked around the corner of the house he was hit from behind and was being dragged toward a car as he regained consciousness and started struggling with the man and managed to free himself as the man jumped in his car and drove away.

Richard never told Leona how close she came to being hurt or maybe killed or what happened to him that night he knew for certain who ever had murdered Daryl was after her to. Leona got up bright and early the next morning and cooked breakfast for Jerry and heard him in the shower she was taking some toast out of the toaster.

When she turned around she threw the toast, plate and all in the air saying Jerry what's wrong with you scaring me like that and he laughed saying shook you up huh, that's the way to get the heart pumping in the morning.

She took his plate from the table and threw his food in the trash saying laugh now sucker as he tried to get her food from her and she told Jerry he was hurting her as he let go of her she ran into her bedroom with her food calling out sucker and broke out into laughter.

Jerry chuckled saying just you wait; pay back is coming to you Jerry was in the kitchen grumbling something and Leona told him to sit down.

Leona told him she would fix him more food he looked at her and said forget it you done got me angry now as she looked at him she started sticking out her tongue.

He smiled and said don't bother he knew how to cook and he said he was always a better cook than her, she told him she would get even with him for that.

They joked around until he told her they better get going if he was going to drop her off at their moms and she said I'm driving and he said not this time as he daggled his car keys in front of her and ran to the car.

She didn't argue this time she just got in the car and they drove off when they arrived at her mom's house she saw her mother wasn't up yet and told Jerry to go ahead and leave she would be fine, walking up on the porch, she took her gun from out from under her shirt dropping down the clip to make sure it was full of bullets then put it away and she sat on the swing saying a prayer, asking God to protect her mother and her brother. She had set there for almost an hour, when she saw her mother walking into the kitchen, looking through the window, and saw some had just went be the window in the kitchen and thought to herself, that she was just seeing things that aren't there. Leona knocked on the door and her mother was surprised to see Leona back so soon, but didn't ask any questions, she was just glad she was there. She helped her mother with her breakfast, then cleaned up the kitchen after her mother ate and asked her if she would like to go shopping, her mother said that was a splendid idea, she told Leona to go back the car out of the garage, she would get dressed, unlike Leona she wasn't five minutes getting dressed and came out the door locking it behind her, waked to the car and got in. Leona saw a glimpse of something moving in the back of the garage and told her mother she would be right back getting out of the car and started walking to the back of the garage she started waking around the corner when she was grabbed and started to scream when she saw it was Richard and asked him what was he trying to do put her in a early grave she said you are going to stop following me, I cant take this anymore if he wants to kill me let him just don't let me see you following me any more. Leona went back to the car. It had been years since these two had shopped together, both of them were looking forward to it. Leona told her mother they were going to have lunch with Jerry, her mother told her not to count on that, Jerry had a tendency of forgetting things, saying she would be lucky if he even went to work that day, she said he has been dating some girl and spends most of his awakening hours with her, Leona said it sounds like its getting serious, I can't believe he hasn't told me. Who is this lucky girl and she said, I think its one of Daryl's friends sister, you remember the boy Daryl went to collage with, he came by her about a year ago asking about Daryl and said he was sorry to hear he had been killed, he had his sister with him and said her name was Lyn or Linda I'm not sure. Leona said mom try to remember, what did he look like, she said honey the only thing I remember, the young man was about Daryl's age, height and build and I noticed he was wearing make up, it struck me in an odd way, she said he noticed me looking at his face and said he had acne, I told him that wasn't anything to worry about, they could cure that, I told him not to drink to many colas, it would clear up in no time. She said Leona why this sudden interest in your brothers girl friend, she said nothing mom, I was just curious, we wont mention it again, she said alright honey, then started talking about a recipe she wanted to try. Leona was anxious to tell Richard and it was aggravating she had to wait for him to contact her. It had been a wonderful morning for Leona and her mother, they about walked there legs off shopping, Leona found a dress she really liked, they went by the car lot where her brother worked, their mother waited in the car, while Leona went inside to see if Jerry was ready for lunch, she saw a young woman sitting in his office, she walked up to the door, her brother was on the phone and motioned for her to come in, when he hung up he said sis, I got a surprise for you, I want you to meet my girl friend Lyn, I invited her to have lunch with us, Lyn said I hope this is alright, I told him I didn't want to impose, Leona said don't be silly any friend of my brothers, is a friend of mine, she said we need to get going mother is waiting in the car. When they got to the car Jerry and his girl friend got in the back seat, Lyn said I see some one has been doing some shopping, Leona said have we ever, I found the prettiest dress and found mom a comfortable pair of shoes, it has been years since we had went shopping, now your putting the icing on the cake, I'm glad you decided to come with us to lunch. Lyn said I can't wait to see your dress, Leona said why should you, take it out of the bag, then said isn't it the prettiest dress you ever saw, Lyn said it sure is, but where would you wear it and Leona said as soon as my brother gets me a date, he will half to take me to a nice place. I'll tell you what lets make it a foursome, I have let go of the past, now the attractive men better look out, Leona's on the prow. Leona's mother said you'll half to look over my daughter, she has been acting like a collage girl again, Lyn said I think that's wonderful. Leona knew this girl and who her husband is; Leona only hoped she was buying her story. Lyn said Leona your face seems so familiar to me, have we meet? Leona said it's possible but she said for the life of me I can't remember, if we had or when. Lyn said she was at hers and Daryl's wedding, Leona thought she would die, Leona said well you understand why I can't remember you, there was four hundred people at my wedding, I only got to meet some of Daryl's friends briefly and said I'm so sorry I don't remember you being there, Leona said, it has been going on fifteen years ago and Lyn said don't worry about it, I can't remember things from yesterday hardly and started Laughing. Leona thought to herself, either this girl bought her story or she is the best actress she had ever seen. After lunch Leona asked Lyn if she would like to go shopping with her and her mother, she said we are going to make a day of it, Lyn told her to give her a rain check, she had to fix dinner for her and Jerry this evening, she hadn't got to the grocery store yet, she was making Lasagna for him and Leona said that was Daryl's favorite dish, but he never really liked the way I made it, but never complained when I did, but one thing is for sure, I don't need to worry about fixing that dish again, then started laughing and Jerry said that's an awful thing to say, Leona said lighten up Jerry, Daryl is dead, I'm moving on, so get use to it. Remember you and mom used to worry me to death to move on with my life now that I am you can't stand it so brother dear make up your mind what's it going to be, do I become a nun or someone's sweetheart, you tell me what you want me to do Jerry. Lyn said you really are over him aren't you. Leona said I'll always love him but face it, he cant keep my bed warm anymore, I just have to find a guy that will, her mother said, Leona you should be ashamed and Leona said oh momma please forgive me for wanting to warm up my sheets and was laughing so hard tears came to her eyes, her mother said jut take me home, if you want to act like a little tramp. Leona said mom where is your since of humor, I swear I should have stayed out west. Lyn was in the back seat laughing at Leona's mother and told Leona she was so funny. Jerry came in from work the next day and said to Leona, that he hoped she was happy. Leona said why all the sarcasm, he said Lyn called him and said she didn't like the way I treated you, she wasn't going to allow any man to talk to her as he did to his sister and told him they were through, that she was leaving town. He walked into his bed room saying, you and your hot sheets. Leona would like to have told him why she acted that way, but knew she couldn't, as she walked into her room in tears, started packing her suite case. It broke her heart knowing her brother despised her; she couldn't stay there for another minute, only she didn't know what to do. She was sitting there crying her eyes out, when her brother came into her room, sat down beside her on the bed, pulled her next to him saying he was sorry, he didn't want to hurt her and said sis please forgive me, don't leave, I will make it up to you some how, she said do you mean it, he said sure I do. Leona looked at him and said sucker, drying up her tears, ran out of the room, as Jerry started screaming at her, saying you big fake, she said Jerry I'm sorry I love you and said please forgive me, he said there's nothing to forgive, its her lose and walked to the refrigerator, saying what's for dinner. Leona went in the kitchen and told him to relax she would fix him his favorite meal, he said you are, just what is that going to be, she said food silly, you will eat anything as long as there is a lot of it, he said a woman that understands me and it has to be my sister. Leona broke out into laughter as Jerry left for work, he thought he would turn the tables on Leona he knew she wouldn't like him to bring a man home to meet her, a sparkle came in his eyes and he knew just the man.

There was a very shy man that worked at the car lot, he was only about five foot four, weighed about two hundred pounds, he couldn't wait to take him home, just to see Leona's face. Jerry pulled in the drive way, when they got out Leona seen what he was up, she went to her bedroom, she put her head under the faucet soaking her hair, then wrapped a towel around her head, when they got inside Jerry said sis come here quick and she came out with a towel wrapped around her and said what is it Jerry, he said I got someone here I want you to meet, he said Tiny this is my sister, Leona walked over to him saying you're the man of my dreams, come here and grabbed him laying a smothering kiss on him, saying come with me to my bedroom, I'm so hot for you. Jerry had never seen this guy move so fast in the five years they worked together, out the door he went running down the street, Leona went running out the door, throwing her towel back inside, saying don't leave I need your body, Jerry went running after her, thinking she went crazy, running out the door naked, saying Leona wait, put this towel back around yourself throwing it out the door, when he got on the porch, Leona was standing with her two piece bathing suit on and said its bad a girl can't get a fellow theses days, throwing the towel in his face, walked back in the house, that was the last time Jerry ever bought a guy home to meet her. Leona was setting on the sofa, she heard a knock at the door and saw it was someone from the wire service, she went to the door and the man told her, there is a telegram for a Leona Moonie, she said that's me, he had her to sigh for the telegram, she opened it and it said keep up the good work you are still being watched, she walked back to the door and saw a car sitting across the street, went back inside and locked the door, saying to herself, when will this ever end. Leona was sitting there half scared to death and then she started to get angry, saying I have had enough, if he wants to get me fine, I'm not going to be afraid anymore. She went outside and got Jerry's riding lawn mower and started mowing the lawn, she had asked Jerry to do it over a week earlier, when she finished, she started weeding the flower beds and then got the trimmer out and started cutting the hedges, when she finished she knew Jerry was going to be angry, there wasn't much of the hedges left after she had got through with them and then she went for the water hose spraying off the porch and drive way. Seeing the window rolled down in the car across the street walked to the end of the drive way and started spraying the person in the car and laughed at him as he started the car and left. Richard pulled in her driveway a few minutes later and told her she wasn't funny the man was just doing his job keeping an eye on her, she turned the water hose on him and walked to the side of the house and washed all the widows and was putting everything away when Jerry drove into the driveway, he looked at the lawn and then her, didn't say a word just went inside the house. Sat down on the sofa then turned on the television, when Leona came in he threw her a set of car keys, she said why are you giving me your keys, he said look again and said those are your car keys and she said you bought me a car, he said of course I did, you didn't think I would let you drive mine forever did you and said get ready we will go and get it. Leona told him just to give her a minute and she would get dressed, Jerry knew how long her minute would be, figuring he would take a nap, two hours later Leona woke him up and said your very funny I told you I would only be a minute, as she was walking out the door, he was surprised not to see her under the steering wheel, he said Leona you can drive if you like, she said now why would I want to do that, your not driving mine. Jerry just shook his head as he got in the car, they past up the car lot where he worked, then proceeded to another car lot and she said why didn't you buy me a car where you work, he said that's not what I wanted to get you, he said you remember when you wanted a car for Christmas, how you cried because I got one instead, she said Jerry I was just a kid then, he said you still act like a kid at times, so quit changing the subject, I always felt guilty about it any way, so Merry Christmas sis and pointed to a brand new Mercedes – Benz convertible. Leona broke down in tears, Jerry said what did I do now, she said nothing you big goof, I'm just happy that's all, he looked at her and said women, I will never understand them, she said your not suppose to, just love us. Leona got inside and put the top down on her car then said thank you Jerry, I love it then got out of her car and Jerry ran, saying you're not kissing on me, just get in your car. Leona laughed at him bumping his head, as he got in his car. Leona told Jerry she would need for him to send for Nebraska Plates, Jerry said he had all ready ordered them for her, they would be there at the end of the week. Leona backed up and went around him, he smiled when he saw the license plate that said hot chick one and Leona thought how lucky she was to have a brother like Jerry. Two weeks has went by and Leona can't figure why Richard hadn't contacted her, she had a lot to tell him, it was starting to get to her, no matter how hard she tried not to be scared, she kept finding herself looking over her shoulder and wished if something was going to happen, that it soon would, at least one way or the other she wouldn't be scared anymore. Leona had went to her mothers and was looking through her photo album and ran across the picture of her brothers girl friend, it was Tony Myers who had his arms around her. He had told Daryl they had just been married, Daryl had seen him kiss her and he sent Daryl a picture of them, saying they were married and said Ha, Ha. Both of them were in their twenties and Tony was a collage friend of Daryl's, Leona had only seen them at her wedding briefly, than never saw them again, until she saw his wife with her brother and thinking they had something to do with Daryl's death, but what reason would they have. Leona was getting tired of waiting on Richard to show his face, she thought she would go visit Daryl's grave, she hadn't been there for a very long time, she went by the florist to buy some flowers, just as she had stepped in the door, she heard a voice say you remember me, when she turned around fear swept through her body, as she said Tony, how good to see you again, as she stood trembling and he said is there a special occasion, she said no, not really, I just came by to get some flowers for my brother, he bought me a car the other day, I just wanted to thank him. He said I don't believe I ever met your bother, she said that's too bad I think you would like him. She said I barely recognized you, how long has it been, he said about seventeen years now I think, she said time sure passes by doesn't it, he said you have that right, he said it was good seeing you again and she said you too, as he started to walk away, she said what's the name of that guy you and Daryl used to go fishing with, he said Sam why, she said for him not to tell anyone, she said I used to have a crush on him and he said your kidding, she said no if he would have asked me out I would have said yes in a heart beat , she said don't get me wrong, I cared for Daryl and thought I owed it to him to try and find his killer, but I don't know if he told you but we were getting a divorce, he said no he never told me that, she said well you knew him as well as I did probably, he never would say anything that might make someone take offence to him. I think he may had a tiny yellow streak if you know what I mean, oh I'm sorry she said, I didn't mean to offend you, I know he was your friend, you sometimes just need to tell me to be quiet, I just don't know when to quit talking, he said sounds to me like your just being honest, she said if your in town awhile maybe we can get together and talk about old times, you don't know how lonely it gets especially at my age its hard to get a man to look at me and even harder to get him in the sack and she started laughing. Tony said this is a side of you I never seen before, I didn't know you were so hot blooded, I wish I could stay and chat but I'm leaving town today, so good luck on your man hunt, she said shoot I never get my man and told him again it was good to see him. When he walked away she took a deep breath and held back her tears, she just knew he would see right through her and wondered why he didn't kill her, right then and there. She went inside the flower shop and picked up some flowers and handed the clerk some money, the clerk asked her if she was alright and she said of course why, he said your really shaking, Leona said what's wrong with you haven't you ever seen a person with Parkinson's disease before, the clerk said there is no need to get hostile, she called him a fruit cake, he said get out of my shop you big mouth woman, she said gladly jerk, as she went out the door. Leona went to her car than pulled out of the parking lot, She saw Tony walk into the flower shop, when he came out he was scratching his head, she stopped at the red light, reached for the binoculars in the glove compartment and watched Tony get in his car, saying what a surprise, there sat Lyn beside him, he bent over and it looked like he kissed her, then came out of the parking lot, taking the street leading out of town. Just as she went through the red light, a car started blowing the horn and she looked in her rear view mirror and she saw it was Richard, she pulled over in the parking lot of a Kroger store and said where have you been, as he approached her car, he said following you and she said did you see that guy I was talking to and Richard said the one you were flitting with and she said what ever, he is the one who killed Daryl and he

said what makes you think that, she told him the whole story and he
said to her, that she was lucky he didn't kill her and she said well he
could have, it's a good thing I'm a decent liar or you would be
following me to the morgue and he said why would I want to do
that, there wouldn't be any more he could do for her then, she
drawled back to slap his face and he grabbed her arm and kissed her
and said I have wanted to do that ever since I met you, she told him
this was no time for romance, if he wanted to get frisky to find a
woman of the night and said your time would be better spent getting
that murderer don't you think, , Richard knew she would like to have
shot him and was glad she didn't have a gun or she would have, and
hope the news he was about to tell her would calm her down.
Richard said his men has been following Tony ever since she got back
in Ellisville and their following him now, if he comes back I'll know
about it, she said I wish you would fill me in sometime. Richard said
if the opportunity rises I most certainly will and she said are you sure
we are taking about the same thing and told him to get his mind out
of the gutter, he just smiled and waked away. Leona didn't know if
Richard was taking her serious and she had a gut felling he would
some how try to keep her away if he got enough evidence to pick
Tony up and that was one thing she wouldn't allow she wanted to
kill him herself if indeed he was guilty of killing Daryl. This time
Leona was going to follow Richard, she watched him go into a motel,
she sat there for hours, then saw him pull out of the parking lot and
she followed him all over Ellisville and when she least expected it,
she was surrounded by cars and Richard walked up to her car, saying
have you followed me long enough and he said I suggest you go back
to your brothers and she said I have been a target for you long
enough, if you don't want to go after the murderer I will, so get these
cars out of my way before I mess up my pretty car my brother bought
me, I swear I'll ram them, do you hear what I am telling you and he
told his men to move back, he said we can pick up her body before
long and she said your right, it is my body and burnt rubber as she
drove off. Richard told his men to keep an eye on her and if she got
hurt, they would be no place they could hide from him. Leona was
hurt that Richard seemed to think he could patronize her, she knew
her instincts were correct when it came to Lyn and Tony, she didn't

know why they wanted to kill her husband she only felt they had or knew who did, if she give this kind of reasoning to Richard he probably would say she needed more than a woman's intuition, but no matter what he thought she knew she had to see it through to the end, she only hope he would keep following her and be there to help her when there true motivations showed its ugly face. Leona had to have someone who believed in her, once again she felt all alone not knowing how to go about proving what she knew to be the truth or who to turn to for help. She returned to Jerry's home and slowly walked up the porch steps felling sick inside, the emptiness returned and she wished Daryl was there, he would trust her and stick by her no matter what, it wouldn't have matter to him if she didn't have all the answers, at least he would support her and now his gone who would even think of doing that for her and she realized there was no one she could turn to and tears stated trickling down her face, as her heart was breaking all over again as she thought about Richard thinking he was the only person who cared enough to listen to her and found out his only interest was in her body and not thinking she had something more important to offer a mind. Leona walked to the door and unlocked it and stepping inside she heard something behind her as she turned she saw it was Richard still filling hurt she told him to go away and he said Leona I believe you and she didn't respond, he said can't you hear me I said I believe you. She looked at him with tears flowing like water and said all you want is to get in my pants get away from me you filthy pig. He looked at her as if she had shot him and said that's not the whole truth I am attracted to you but I know you're a very intelligent woman and I'm sorry for treating you the way I did, she said you had your chance now stay away from me, your fired get off my husbands case she said you disgust me and screamed for Jerry as Richard turned and walked away. Leona had fallen to her knees as Jerry came on the front porch he said what's wrong sis as he helped her to her feet and she put her arms around him murmuring his gone, as she placed her head on his shoulder and was crying letting lose all the hurt that was in her and said Jerry, what am I going to do and kept on crying as he took her in the house, when Jerry got her inside and shut the door Richard stepped out of the shadows saying, I am truly sorry Leona I will make this right and turned and walked away. The next morning Leona looked out the window and saw something setting on the porch and walked out to see what it was, she saw a note that was on the top of it saying this is a copy of everything I have at my disposal, I only hope you will change your opinion of me and gave her a number where he could be reached and said please accept my apology, it was signed Richard. Jerry came out side and said what's all of this and she said the pieces to a puzzle and said help me carry all this in the house and he said where in the world will we put it all, there must be a truck load and Leona said quit acting like a little boy and get started. Richard stood and watched as they removed everything from the front porch and smiled and got in his car and drove off. Leona looked out the window and said thank you for believing in me and Jerry said who are you talking to, she said a very dear man and Jerry said I'm sorry I asked looking at her as if she had went bananas and she said your welcome and started going through the paper work, Jerry told her it would take a year to go through all those paper she said are you going somewhere and he just laughed and said how can I help. Leona told him what she was looking for and he said well sis if its in here we will find it, she bent over and kissed him on the cheek and he said if your going to get mushy then I'm going to spend the day at moms house and she said did you say something and he repeated him self and she did to and they both broke out laughing. They worked all through the day and half the night and Jerry said sis, this is like trying to run a hundred yard dash, only you twisted your ankle before you got started, she said I know the felling but I know the answer is here some where, so lets look in the last place we would look and go from there, Jerry said that's the smartest thing I ever heard you say, she said I knew you would like it and both of them started empting paper all over the floor and Jerry thought he had found a good system, he was saying Enee mini mighty Moe and then look at the papers and threw them over his shoulder. Leona looked at him and asked what he thought he was doing, saying don't you realize how important these papers are, they hold the key that will unlock the mystery behind Daryl's death, so quit fooling around. Jerry held his head down poked his lip out and said yes mother and Leona flipped her lid saying you rotten, self centered, egotistical, spoiled brat, a poor excuse for a man, how dare you take this lightly, Jerry was backing away from her saying, now sis I was only playing, you wouldn't do something drastic now would you, as he saw her starting to boil and he sprang to his feet and was running for his life, how could he ever explain getting beat up by his sister, it hadn't worked when he tried as a boy and it sure would be worse now that he is a man and as angry as Leona was, he knew she wouldn't care what she hit him with, only this time he didn't have his mother to protect him, as he ran out the door saying I'll be back later when you cool down. Leona was so tired she decided to try and get some sleep as she walked into her bed room and fell across her bed. Leona woke up several hours later and saw Jerry had put all the papers back in order and had his head laying on his arm propping his self up on the table fast a sleep, Leona went over and kissed him on the check as he jumped up falling off his chair saying, sis please don't be angry anymore. She said your safe brother as he gave a sigh of relief and she told him to go get some sleep and he said he couldn't he just had enough time to take a shower and get to work. He looked at Leona and said I never took what you are doing lightly , I'm sorry for the way I carried on, you know I always do stupid stuff when I'm tired, we have been at it for nearly twenty hours. Leona told him she was sorry two he was a good man and he said what about the rest of the things you said and she said don't push it brother as he threw up his hands and said I surrender. Leona started laughing at him and said get in the shower and he didn't say a word just went to do as he was told. Leona didn't hear the shower running and went to check on Jerry, he had done as she did, fell across the bed and was a sleep as soon as he lay down. Leona called his job and told them he had been up all night with a friend and she said you could call it a sick one and said thank you for understanding as she hung up the phone. Leona was looking at some papers she thought may help in the investigation and decided to call Richard, but didn't really know what to say to him, she knew she had hurt him, and it wasn't easy for her to apologies, but she would do what ever was necessary to bring Daryl's murders to justice. Leona called Richard and asked him to come by Jerry's house and told him she needed to talk to him, she started to apologies and she said alright then and hung up the phone, it was nearly eight hour before Richard arrived, he knocked on the door and Jerry went to the door and told him to come in, he walked in the kitchen and saw Leona going through more of the papers and he said what was it you needed me to look at. Leona told him of a place where Daryl and his collage buddies used to go fishing, she said Daryl had told her once that he had a locker there where he kept all his fishing gear and she said when I noticed this papers, telling of the areas in witch they went fishing, I happened to remember the locker, I don't know if it means any thing but I would like to check out this locker to see what's there, and asked Richard what he thought, he said if its important enough to arouse suspicion, then I think we need to go there and have a look, they may be something there you would like to keep, she looked into Richard eyes and said you do trust my intuition, he said I made that mistake once, not trusting, it won't happen again and he said how soon can you be ready to go and she told him she was already packed and their tickets were already paid for, he said where are we going and she said to the gulf coast of Texas to a town called Portland and the locker is at Crusoe Riggers. Jerry drove them to the air port and he told Richard to take care of her and Richard told him she was a big girl and she knew how to take care of herself. It was eleven thirty that night when the plane landed in San Antonio and they would fly from there to Corpus Christi rent a car and dive to Portland. It was tree thirty pm the next day before they got to Portland, when they went into Crusoe Riggers, Leona told them she wanted to get the things from her husbands locker after she told them her name and showed them her drivers license, they said it was no problem if she could tell them the locker number. Leona said look at your files, how am I to know what locker number, I'm his wife not a mind reader, She looked at Richard and he said don't you know the number and the clerk smiled and said if you don't lady then we can't help you, she said give me a second I'll think of it and the clerk said we don't deal here in guessing games, if you don't give me the right number right off, then I'm sorry we can't allow you to look in his locker. She smiled and said give me the key to number one hundred thirty eight, he looked in his book and said you did know his number, come with me, when they reached the locker he unlocked the door and said if you all need anything I'll be at the desk handed her the Key and told her to keep it and walked away. When Leona open the locker she saw a full blown up picture of her in a bikini taped to the locker door and she smiled and took it down, Richard said he didn't only have good taste in women, but also in fishing tackle, he said look at this stuff he was a serious fisherman, Leona took several pairs of ray band sun glasses from the locker shelf that had Monday through Sunday written on their cases she found a set of keys and a captains hat on the shelf and a metal box that was filled with pictures and on the top was a picture of a boat and she could see there was a name on it butt couldn't make out the name, she handed it to Richard and she said what does all this mean and Richard said your husband was more than a fisherman that came here to charter a boat I think maybe he owns one to, she said your kidding and he said no I'm not, look at this and showed her the title to a boat that was in her name. He had finished paying it off two months before he was killed and this is no small boat Richard said. Showing her a picture of the boat and it had Leona written on the back. She said I wonder why he didn't tell me and Richard said maybe he didn't get a chance, he probably was going to surprise you or why else would he have put in your name. Richard said what do you want to do with all this stuff and she said for now we will leave it and pointed to a small tackle box and said I take that one with me and he said why this one and she said look at the number on it, when Richard looked he saw it had the number one hundred thirty eight Leona closed the locker and locked it back with the key the clerk handed her and told Richard she wanted to see the boat and he said I'm with you, I want to see it myself. She went to the clerk and asked him to show her the boat her husband had bought and he said your in luck it was docked here two days ago and she said by whom and he said by a man named Tony Myers, he had a note from your husband saying he could use the boat and she said my I see the note and he said, I'm sorry, but I gave it back to him. He said is there a problem she said no she was just curious her husband forgot to mention it. She told him if Tony came in again not to say she was even there, she said I wouldn't want to embarrass him, you know put him in the middle and he told her his lips were sealed and said come with me I'll show you the boat.

When Richard saw the boat he said this is a fisherman's dream and
Leona said yea she thought she could get used to it and told Richard
they would half to come back and spend some time on the boat.
 I'm sure Jerry wouldn't mind coming with us and Richard just
smiled. Leona asked the clerk how much it cost a month to dock the
boat there and he said nothing, when a boat is purchased from us we
give a lifetime of free docking.
She said that's great and he said yes it is a good package and she said
what happens if you all should happen to close down and he said our
company is held responsible for other docking arrangements.
 Its all in our contract with the buyer and she said may I have a copy
of mine and he said of course I'll get one for you, after looking at the
contract not only did Daryl get free docking his locker was included
and everything is insured for five years.
Leona was pleased with there results and she knew for certain Tony
had bought her story and she told Richard they would get on the
next flight out.
It was midnight the following day before Leona walked upon the
porch to Jerry's home.
 Richard was returning back to Chicago, she unlocked the door and
stepped inside turned on the light and was making her way into the
kitchen when her brother stepped out and she froze.
 She said what are you doing in here in the dark, he told her he was
getting a piece of chicken that he was hungry and she said you got
any more and he replied sure thing and went to get her some.
It dawned on her the kitchen was empty.
She shouted out "where are all my papers!" He replied relax sis they
are safe I just put them in a place where you could work better that's
all and she replied I liked working here and he smiled saying he
knew she did but this was his home not her office so he got her one
asking her to stop shouting at him before he went deaf.
She replied I'm sorry Jerry its been a rough four days and he said
that's alright sis I know this is taking a toll on you, so I got you
something and she said you did what, he walked out of the room and
came back handing her a trophy with a woman statue on top and she
said why would you give me this, he said why don't you read the

inscription and she laughed, it read Leona defender of truth and justice.

She started to walk toward him and he said can't you accept something with out slobbering on a fellow, she said Jerry your to much.

He told Leona he was going back to bed and as he walked passed, he said you're getting a little fat there aren't you sis, as he felt a sudden breeze go by his head and saw her shoe hit the wall and he ran into his bedroom. Leona woke up the next morning hearing a lawn mower and saw Jerry was on his tractor, she went in the kitchen and fixed breakfast and called Jerry in to eat, he parked the tractor beside the house and came in the kitchen door and said something smells wonderful and Leona said its called food and he said I knew that as he sat down at the table piling food on his plate, Leona told him if he ate all that he couldn't get up and he said hush woman let a man eat in piece and ducked as the toast came fling at him and he said hit the plate not the head she told him she was surprised he didn't catch the toast in mid air since he was wolfing down his food and he said cute Leona and kept on eating. After she had cleaned up the kitchen she asked him where he put her papers and he said follow me and went outside and pointed at the garage and she said you think I would be more comfortable in your garage, he said it was either there or the picnic table, besides you haven't seen your office yet. He told her the crew had just finished it late last night as she walked toward the garage she saw that a door way had been put in, on the back side of the building and when she went inside, she told Jerry it was beautiful he had everything an office could need in it, including a refrigerator and microwave she told him this was so thoughtful of him and he said I wanted room for you a bed but I figure I would be stretching it a little and she said Jerry don't you want me to stay with you, you're my favorite brother, he said aren't I the lucky one, since I'm the only sibling you have. She went over and picked up the phone and he said who are you calling, I suggest you stick your head out the door and holler real loud, maybe they will hear you, your phone wont be connecter until the first of the week, but never fret he said and handed her a cord to her phone and said I ran this from the house for you, I just wanted to get the lawn mowed first. She asked Jerry where he got the long cord and he said that was easy, he used her credit card, no problem. She said you used my credit card, he said how do you think I got all this stuff, mine is maxed out. Leona started screaming Jerry, as he took off running, to the front of the house. Leona gave Richard a call and asked him if he had the contents of Daryl's locker from the school, he told her no he didn't, she said she had the recite for it, there were supposed to be a key in it and his books, pictures, a knife, a gym bag, pair of sweets, tennis shoes and several other items. Richard told her he would check in on it, he said if you have the recite the things had to be somewhere he would find them, he said is it something important and she said only the key she said, she thought maybe it was to her father-in-laws cabin, she said she didn't have the key and as particular as he is, he would get very angry if he knew a key was missing, she said Daryl had left a few things there and she would like to go get them and asked if he could pick a lock that she didn't want to half to ask him for a key, if she could help it. He told her he would be in Ellisville at the end of the week. Leona decided she wasn't going to wait on him she would get Jerry to go with her and see if they could get inside, Jerry had got off work that evening about five pm. It was six thirty and he hadn't made it home yet, that was unusual for Jerry he was always prompt, Leona called his work and they told her he left that morning he said his sister called and said his mother was in the hospital and told him to get there as fast as he could, they said he ran to his car and got in it and took off. Leona started shaking as she called Richard and told him what Jerry's company told her, she said she was really worried she hadn't told him about his ex-girl friend and was worried that she might have been the one who called him and if that were true Tony was back in Ellisville. Richard said he isn't in Ellisville he is in Laredo Texas, he said it sounded to him like her brother made up a story to get out of work and he would have his staff to find him and told her not to worry, he felt sure he was in no danger and she told him she hoped he was right. Two day has past and Leona hadn't heard a word from Jerry, she was getting worried sick and she didn't know where to begin to look for him, she said to her self if he isn't hurt he is going to be when he gets home. Richard called Leona and said his staff had looked all over Ellisville and they even checked at your moms and he wasn't there he said he must have somewhere he snuck off two and if he wasn't there by the next day for her to call the police and put in a missing person report and he told her he would be arriving that night, his plane should land around nine thirty and he would see her at Jerry's home sometime there after. When Richard arrived Leona was still in her office working, Richard walked in the back of the house and called out to her he didn't want to frighten her and she answered I'm in the garage come to the door on the side. Leona was opening the door as Richard walked up and he said are you alright and she said I'm fine thank you for asking, Richard said I have this crazy notion I know where your brother might be and she said clue me in and he said my staff did deliver Daryl's things here from his locker and I got a hunch your brother is at that cabin, Leona said I'll kill him and Richard said lets do something better than that and she said what do you have in mind, after he told her they both about rolled on the floor with laughter. Richard made a phone call putting his plan into action and he said if we hurry we can watch all the fun. Richard and Leona arrived at the cabin at four am and parked there car almost a quarter mile a way and Richard said it ought to be going down any minute now and if he is in that cabin he will never pull a stunt like this again. Leona's father-in -laws cabin was well secluded there wasn't another cabin within twenty miles Richard and Leona was ready for the action to begin, they heard the helicopter flying in, saw the men slide down on ropes and surrounded the cabin, Leona thought that Jerry wasn't there, the noise from the helicopter would have awaken her but there wasn't a sound in the cabin, but after the men started beating on the side of the cabin, the lights came on and Jerry was the first they grabbed taken him out of the cabin along with two other men and six women, they were all drunk as skunks the men started tying them all to a tree and Jerry keep telling them to have a drink, but when Richard's men started stripping the men down to their underwear, all the drunks started sobering up, when they got sober, the sun had started coming up, the men that Richard sent in was talking gibberish and Leona was laughing so hard she thought she was going to have a heart attack, the men let everyone go except Jerry and they said someone had to pay for breaking into the cabin, they took Jerry beside the cabin, after he saw eight men standing in front of him with rifles, they put a blind fold on him and asked if he had any last request, you never heard a man cry so loud, begging them not to kill him, Leona walked down to the men and said real loud get ready aim and fire, as the riffles went off Jerry fell to his knees saying he was sorry, Leona went over to him and took the blind fold off and said now worry me again, as everyone broke out laughing even the friends he took with him, Leona untied him and he said how could you do this to me, I swear I'll get even and she said alright then if you hadn't had enough and he said I take it back Leona, please, just let me go home and she said I planed to brother and told him his car was parked at the end of the road and all the others that were with him started laughing at him and Leona said you all think this is funny huh looking at the men and winked, she said you men deserve a reward, have your way with them and when the men started walking toward the women, they took off running down the road saying this is not funny. The helicopter had landed a few hundred yards away in a clearing and the men headed for the Helicopter and Leona went inside the cabin and called for her brother to clean the place up before he left and looked around and got the things that belonged to Daryl and left the cabin and told Jerry she would see him at home not to make her come after him. When Jerry got home he went to Leona and told her that was the worst thing she had ever done to him and she said you don't think taking Daryl's things was bad and going to his dads cabin to lay four days drunk was bad and making me worry sick, telling your job our mother was in the hospital. Jerry said your right Leona I deserved what I got, he said do we have a truce and she said sure why not and they gave each other a hug and Richard said he was glad everything worked out all right and Jerry walked over and went up beside his head with his fist and said you talked her into doing that and Richard got up and said your right I did then decked him only Jerry didn't get up Richard had knocked him out. Leona said that boy will never learn and said thank you Richard for teaching him a lesson in more ways than one and kissed him and he pulled her back to him and kissed her again and she said slow down fellow I'm grateful but not that grateful and Richard just laughed. Jerry was coming around and looked at Richard and then at Leona and said am

I interrupting something and Leona said what do you mean, nothing I guess I just didn't know Richard wore your shade of lipstick, he hits hard for a girl and Leona helped him to his feet and asked him if he was alright, he answered I will be if you keep the gorilla off me, Richard answered and let him know he shouldn't let his hands do what his face has to pay for and Jerry said I got the message, only this time when he hit Richard he put his lights out and said I never do and walked away. Leona just looked at her brother in shock and thought to her self where did it go Jerry and she looked at her brother in a different light, he had become a man and she never again referred to him as boy. Richard woke up and asked Leona what happened and she told him her brother just introduced himself, as Richard started rubbing his Jaw and replied I would have never thought and Leona spoke up and said what, that he couldn't knock you on your can, well say hello to Jerry, that is if your not to scared to. Richard said women, and Leona said did I hurt your little bittie feelings and he said knock it off we have work to do and she just smiled. Jerry had came out of the office and said look at this you two and showed them a picture of Daryl and three Men on a Fishing boat and Jerry asked Leona who the guy was that had rosacea and Leona said I have no idea, Richard said let me look at that, he said I've seen this picture and I thought it was a sun burn he said, Jerry you just figured out what Daryl was trying to tell us when he wrote crimson with his blood, when we figure out who the man is in the picture, then we will know who killed Daryl. Leona said are you nuts Daryl didn't write rosacea, but in a way he did Richard said the word crimson means, redness in the face or make something become this color, don't you get it he couldn't spell rosacea so he wrote something that described it. Richard said I know this sounds far fetched, but I will stick my reputation on it I'm right. Leona said how does this explain Lyn dating my brother when she is married to Tony and Jerry said what are you talking about Leona, Lyn is Tony sister and Leona said how do explain me seeing her with him and he kissed her on the mouth and Jerry laughed and said there whole family does that, they kiss each other that don't make them killers and besides I like when her sisters greeted me, its odd but nice. Leona said they came to my wedding and Tony said she was his wife and Jerry said someone must have seen them kissing and instead of them trying to explain he said she was his wife, I heard him say the same thing and when people turned their back they would break out laughing. I know sis it's weird but true, this goes back to their grand parents, and they are the closest family I ever saw and he said the first thing came into my mind was incest, but I assure you that's not the case. Leona looked at Richard and Richard said don't worry I will keep them under surveillance. Jerry kept looking at the picture and said I know this place and Leona said where is it and Jerry said give me a minute to think, I have seen this background before, he said it was in Ocean City Maryland, I went there once on a convention and this boat shouldn't be to hard to find look here and he pointed to the name of it, the Dolphin. When Leona looked at Richard he said I'm on the same page with you, we will get the next flight out. Leona and Richard flew into the Dulles airport in Washington DC and rented a car and drove to Ocean City Maryland they checked in at a Motel and Leona was walking on the board walk only six hours after they left Ellisville, while Richard and some of his staff were checking all the docks to find the Dolphin. Two days had past and no one had found the charter that Daryl and his friends were on. Leona was starting to think Jerry was mistaken about the location where they were at, she thought she knew who all Daryl's friends were and couldn't understand why she didn't recognize the person in that picture. Leona knew she had been through about all the pictures and looked at all the material Richard had given her, but it seemed like they hadn't come any closer to the person that killed her husband and she started wonder if they ever would. Leona decided to call Jerry and have him look at the picture again and to concentrate harder on it, she wanted him to be absolutely sure that they were searching in the right area, it had been twenty years since that picture was taken and she thought to herself peoples looks do change and she was thinking maybe ones memory does to. Leona didn't know Jerry had taken such an interest in the investigation it was four days before she finally reached him at home he had been in her office looking through the paper work to see if any of it made since to him, but he told Leona he was clueless and got more confused the longer he went through them, he said I cant remember where I started or where I left off, he said he was just going to leave it to the professionals he had enough, however he did tell her he was certain that they were in the right location, because out of all the conventions he had went to, it was there where he stayed sober and really enjoyed himself. Richard returned to the motel that evening and told Leona that they found the boat it had been setting in dry dock for the last five years he said the owner of the boat had died, but he was able to talk to the captain and I learned more about your husband than I realized I would, after showing him Daryl's picture he said he remembered him as though it were yesterday, he said he was the only blind man he ever took fishing and said his name was Hook. I didn't know it at the time, but I found out later he was in the last stages of Alzheimer Disease. Richard told her his staff was still working on finding some of the people who worked on the boat but didn't think they would find anything. Leona said lets go out and get some sea food I heard they had some of the best in the world right here; at least it won't be a wasted trip and Richard agreed. They left the next morning to return to Ellisville, Leona asked Richard did he really think he could solve this case and he told her he was a patient man and there was no doubt in his mind, after all he said I got you helping me and if I can't solve this one then I'll pack it in and I'm a long way from giving up. Leona's mother came to visit Jerry and Leona they were cooking dinner for her and she asked Leona how the investigation was coming and Leona told her it seemed like it was at a stand still. She picked up the picture of Daryl and his friends on the boat that Jerry had carried in the house and she said there is that handsome young man and Leona smiled and said Daryl was handsome wasn't he and her mother said no not him and yes your right Daryl was handsome to and Leona went behind her mother looking over her shoulder said who are you talking about she said the young man standing beside Daryl, you know the one I told you about and she said your talking about Tony and she said I guess so I thought he had acne I didn't realize he had rosacea, Leona said mom are you sure she said of course I am he came by the house once with Daryl don't you remember, you weren't married to Daryl then and Leona said mom I never saw him and her mother said my mind is starting to slip, you weren't home when Daryl came by if memory serves me, you were with your aunt Becky you remember you had to have your wedding dress altered and I wasn't filling well that day and she went in my stead, I remember it as tough it was yesterday. Leona said mom I do remember and ran out of the kitchen and her mother said what's wrong with that girl and Jerry said mom you just figured out who killed Daryl, she said I did how did I do that and Jerry told her it was a long story and said I be right back as he went out the kitchen door running after Leona. Leona mother said to herself I love them but they both have went crazy, I knew they took after their fathers side of the family and walked to the stove to stir the food. Leona was calling Richard to tell him, when he walked in behind Jerry going in her office and she was saying pick up the phone Richard and he said you got to lay it down first and she turned around in her seat and said you're a funny man when did you get back in town and he said last night, what's up, she said I was right about Tony and my mother just confirmed it and he said what are you talking about she said Tony killed Daryl. Jerry said listen mom was looking at the picture of Daryl on the boat and recognized the man on the boat; it is Tony who has rosacea. Richard said are you sure and Leona said I'm very sure, now go get him and he said what for and she told him because he killed Daryl and Richard said slow down woman, its one thing to know he did but proving it is another. Richard said now we got to trace him back to his collage years and find out what kind of motive he would have for killing Daryl, unless you already know the answer. Leona said Richard I hate it when your right all the time, he said I smelled something good what are we having for dinner, Leona said how can you think about food at a time like this and he said a fellow has got to eat I am starving, am invited or not, she said well of course you are and Richard started walking out the door and she said where are you going and he said I don't think I'm going to get curb service so I think I'll try my luck in the kitchen maybe your mom will feed me and Leona said Richard your impossible as she stormed out of her office. Dinner that evening was good for some and a chore for others, all during dinner Leona frowned at Richard and he just ignored her, when dinner was over she said now your feed, what are you going to do and he said I'm going to watch a little television with Jerry, I hadn't had a chance to watch a movie in months. Leona started to say something when her mother told her to put some of that energy to use and start on the dishes and said leave that poor man alone, can't you see he is completely tuckered out and Leona said your right mom he does look tired and her mother said that's my girl and walked to her and put her arms around her and said don't worry honey he will get him, I can see the determination in his face, Leona said I only hope your right mom as she stared at the picture of Daryl. Leona had finished the dishes and went in the living room and said, where is Richard and Jerry said I don't know I thought he went back in the kitchen with you and mom and Leona walked out on the front porch and saw Richard asleep in the swing, she motioned for Jerry and said you wake him up and let him sleep in my bed and I'll spend the night with mom and Jerry said alright sis if that's what you want to do and she said he could use a good night sleep, just wait until we leave, he looks so comfortable there, Jerry said sometimes you make me want to puke, you and your girlish ways and walked back in the house. Leona arrived back at Jerry's home early, she saw that Richard's car was gone and she asked Jerry what time he left. Jerry said I don't want to talk about it, she said Jerry what did you do and he said nothing sis the jerk woke me up this morning moaning in the shower, she said was he alright, he said anyone that sings like that needs to be shot and put out of their misery. Leona said you need to record yourself sometime, the first time I heard you sing I thought you were calling pigs, he told her she was a barrel of laughs but he had to get to work and managed to kiss her on the cheek on the way out. Leona went to her office and found a note Richard had left and told her he would be in touch if he found out anything and told her not to worry. Richard came back to Jerry's late that evening and told Leona they were barking up the wrong tree, he said that Tony just went back to work, and he told her he was dermatologist and said we went back to his elementary school, high school and collage years, the man never had rosacea, Leona said no that can't be he has to be the one, go back and look again and he said Leona I can't, my people were thorough, he said I no how much you wanted it to be him, but the mans slate is clean and Jerry was telling you the truth about his family, he said I'm sorry and we checked to see if he had a twin and he doesn't. Leona said she didn't care what he said or where he checked Tony killed Daryl and if he would go get him she would and started out the door as Richard grabbed her telling her she wasn't going anywhere. Richard told her he had eliminated him from being a suspect and took the surveillance of him, she said what now, you know I am right you just can't stand it because I figured this out before you did, well swallow you pride buster, I was right, your wrong now live with the fact and go get him or stay out of my way. Richard said, hold your horses Leona, you have such a bad temper that sometimes I fill like putting you across my knee, if you quit acting like a child I have something to tell you. Richard said he has a look alike, he said in this world of ours we all have a look alike, over the years I have seen it time and time again where people were arrest because they favored someone else; the man in the picture with Daryl is not Tony Myers. Leona said what are you talking about that is Tony Myers, my mother even said it was and he said Jerry told him that your mother didn't know his name she just agreed with you that it was his name. Richard said if you will hush I want to show you something. He put a picture up of Tony that was taken twenty years ago and said look at this and look at the picture of his look alike. She said I see they aren't the same man but they look enough alike to be brothers, Richard said your close they are cousins and he is under surveillance as we speak his name is Terry Myers and he does have rosacea and Richard said guess what, Leona said tell me, he is a English teacher at Glenn Dale, New Mexico and the man that killed your husband, now all we have to do is to prove it. Richard told her his wife had died from a long term sickness she had and he moved to New Mexico and never returned to Ellisville. Richard said he was going to check all her medical records and see if he couldn't find out the exact cause of her sickness he was trying to get a court order on the amount of evidence he had so far, but didn't think he had enough and most cases you have to have full proof before a judge would release one. He told Leona to keep looking through the pictures and photos maybe she could come across something, he said I am for certain we will nail this man. Richard was going back to the university were Daryl went, to see if this Terry Myers went to collage with him, he had to find out how and when they met, he also was going to find out everything there was to know about Terry, once he found that out, he could find a motive for him killing Daryl. It didn't take Richard long before he found out that Terry did indeed go to the same collage as Daryl and he was in his sophomore year when Daryl arrived, he was in the same frat house with Daryl he was an excellent student, was never in any trouble. Richard had got in touch with several off his coeds after talking with them, he found out they never knew he was married, and they knew he was seeing a girl by the name off Cindy but the relationship never went any where. Richard knew he had his work cut out for him, he knows Terry was married to a Breanne Thompson, but no one seemed to know when or where they were married and found out her name wasn't anywhere in the university files and no one knew she existed. Richard received word that the court had denied the release of Breanne's medical records, if he could only find who her parents were they could get the medical records and he would also know how old she was at the time of her demise. He decided to go back to Ellisville and see if he could find anyone there who may knew her and where she came from. He returned the next day to Ellisville and found that Leona hadn't found a thing yet on either one of them and Richard had no choice to seek out a relative of Terry's and see if he could get an answer from them, the only problem with that was, he could run a chance of tipping his hand to Terry and if he killed once he would do it again so he had to be careful how he went about asking them. Richard went to the police department to inquire about Terries family, he found out he had two sisters, one had moved away and the other lived outside of Ellisville in a place called Beverly, they told him the girls name that moved away was Tammy Blue and the one that lived in Beverly was Nancy Snyder, with a little home work he found out she worked at a sewing factory, where she was a supervisor, her husband Tommy was an electrician, they had two children both of them girls. Richard decided to put both of them under surveillance and to see what kind of people he was going to be up against. After two week he found out that Tommy was a good man and spent all his time off work being with his daughter, Nancy wasn't lets say a faithful wife and Richard had to find out just how much she cared about her marriage, she was prostituting on the side and the question was did her husband know about it. Richard figured the way he spent time with the girls he had no idea what his wife was doing and Richard was going to take advantage of the situation if possible. Richard didn't like using the tactics he had in mind, but time would tell if her family meant anything to her and after a month of surveillance it seemed she was a good mother despite her extra activities. Richard decided he had to take a chance on who she cared for more her brother or her family. Richard knew from her life style she had to have more money than what her and her husband made and now he believes her husband knows exactly what she is doing, since he found out his business was near bankruptcy just three years prior to now, just about the same time his wife went to work for an escort service and Richard also found out she used to be a striper in Los Vegas while she was attending a business school. Richard discovered her working name was Bridget and arranged a date as they call it at the escort service, she was to meet him at a local night club and the escort arranged a room at one of the finest motels in Ellisville to continue their evening at a cost of two thousand dollars, it seemed she was suppose to be good at what she does. Richard had wished he had one of his staff go on this meeting, it bought back terrible memories to him having had a cheating wife, but he knew how important this was and was going to do whatever it took to get the information out of this woman, even if he had to buy it. Richard was really surprised to see a woman of thirty five that looked like twenty, she was a beauty in every since of the word, he found her to be both witty and funny and she made her presence known to everyone in the club. After dinner and a lot of small talk it was time for them to go to the motel, when the came out of the night club their was a limousine waiting for them and took them directly to the motel and she told the driver she wouldn't be needing his service any longer that night and she told Richard to come with her as she took his hand and walked to their room. Once inside the room you would have thought that a tiger had been turned lose as Richard reached into his inside pocket of his suit and pulled out pictures that were pretty explicate, she looked at the pictures and then said who are you, he then showed her his credentials and she said what is it you want with me, I like you she said and we could have had a good time together and we still can if you tear up those photos, as Richard shoved her away and said I want the you to tell me where Breanne Thompson was from and who her parent are. She said Breanne is dead, why do you want to know and Richard said I'll ask the questions and she said ask, that doesn't mean I'll give you an answer and Richard said I think you will and pulled out some pictures of her daughters and said I know your husband doesn't mind what your doing, but what about your children, when social services takes them away after I have these published. And I know your employer's wife would like to see theses and showed her more pictures, you can kiss the hundred and fifty thousand dollars a year good bye. She said how do I know I can trust you, Richard said how do I know you wont call certain parties that would suffer because of the information I want you to give me, she said I see your point, Richard told her he really didn't care how she lived her life as dangerous as it is, but what I do care about is Breanne. Nancy told him Breanne was an orphan and she was worth more to Terry dead than she was alive, she said I like Breanne, but also liked living, a pretty good trade off for keeping my mouth shut, I told the jerk I wished he never told me about feeding her rat poison a little at a time until it killed her, soon after she died he left and went to New Mexico and I haven't seen him since and if he finds out I told you, your looking at a dead woman. What stopped him from killing you and don't give me the brotherly love story Richard said. Nancy said she had a bargaining tool, a copy of a life insurance policy he had on his wife, Richard said I'll need to have it and she said not on your life, I don't want to lose my children but I have this thing about living and as long as I have that, he wont bother me. Richard said you don't need to worry about him pulling out his gun, and said it's me you need to worry about, now I want that policy or your children are going to be orphans and then he pulled back the hammer on his gun and said you got five seconds. She said I don't have it on me I will take you to it and he said lets go, she said if I walk out of here before morning we are both dead, he said what are you talking about, she said its company policy we are to keep our clients happy and if we leave this room, they will know something is wrong and they would never allow me to talk. Richard said alright then but the first thing in the morning we go get it and told her to take the couch, he paid for the bed and she said why, I could join you and he said don't flatter yourself your not all that. It was eight o'clock the next morning when they left the motel, Richard said what is your routine, she said we have breakfast together and then you kiss be good bye, that shows them you were satisfied with the goods and Richard said fine I pick you up at your home at ten and we will get the policy, if your not there I will find you. She said the sooner this is over the better she would like it. Richard pulled in front of the woman's house, she ran out to his car and got in, she told him to hurry she didn't want her kids to see them and Richard pulled away and he said where to and she said the bank. They only had to go five blocks to her bank and when she returned handed him the policy and he asked her where she wanted to go and she said Switzerland and laughed, she said I'll get out here and call a cab and Richard said you have beautiful children and a piece of free advise stop what your doing and find another way to live I think you'll live longer and then he drove away. Richard drove back to Jerry's house and told Leona what he had found out and said get those files on your husband, there is something I want to check, looking through the papers he said I thought for sure he and then stopped, she said what is it and he said nothing just a hunch, but I see I was wrong and told her he would see her later and told her there was a judge he wanted to see then got in his car and left. Richard got five blocks from Jerry's house when two cars pulled up on each side of him, he noticed Nancy in the back seat of one as a man got out with a gun and told him to give him the insurance papers Richard done as he was asked, the man hit Richard with the gun and got in his car living Richard unconscious, when he woke up the police was by his car and asked him if he was alright and Richard told him he thought he was and they asked him what happened and Richard said I guess the woman's husband didn't like me taking her out, he said I'm fine know and ask them if he could leave and the policeman said sure, just stay away from married women and Richard said I never will do it again and drove off. Richard knew it didn't matter he could have the body exhumed and could get Terry put behind bars, Richard did have the body exhumed only to find an empty casket, the body hadn't been buried, at least not in this grave. It seemed Terry had a diabolical kind of mind it wasn't enough he murdered Linda he took from her a place of rest, if

Richard theory was correct he needed her body to gaze upon as a reward for the hideous crime he had committed. Although disappointed Richard knew it would only be a matter of time before he would put the last pieces to this puzzle together and knew the answers lied somewhere in the last hours of Daryl's life, he had pointed out who killed him and Richard knew somewhere he gave the reason why. Richard had ever detail of what was found in the investigation he had numerous photos, he had went through all the material at least a hundred times, Richard thought to himself that Daryl had offered himself as a ransom for the safety of his family, he knew his chances of getting away was slim at best, he knew the answer had to be in his personal belongings lying in wait for someone to find. Daryl had carefully planed his final hours, leaving clues along the way that wouldn't endanger his family until he could point to his killer. With this mind set Richard returned to Jerry's house no longer would he look through things he already covered all the paper work had been eliminated, once again Richard had to reenact Daryl's life and as the old saying goes he had to walk a mile in his shoes to know the way he thought. Richard told Leona he wanted her to take him back to the last week of the time she spent with Daryl, he wanted to do all the things they were doing together in the last week and Leona told him she thought she could remember but she would only go to a certain point with him, he said her love life hadn't entered his mind, as she looked at him blushing. Leona asked Jerry if he could get some time off work and he asked why she said you remember we went on a fishing trip with Daryl and Jerry said sis you know I hate camping and she said quit your whining can you take off or not, he said give me five minutes and I will find out. Richard told her to think hard he wanted to take everything on this trip as if Daryl was helping you only you will have to instruct me on what he did and she said if you're a fisherman you know what you need and if not we are wasting our time. She said some of his things are in Jerry's garage all the rest is at mothers. As Richard was putting the things in the car, Jerry hollered out the door and said everything is a go. Leona said I'll call mom and tell her to bring over the station wagon and Richard said what for she said we used it to haul all our stuff in, when we went camping. Richard said alright, all he ever took

was a fishing pole, tackle box, sleeping bag, and a lantern. She said
you sound like Daryl, he couldn't talk me into that, neither can you.
It only took four hours to get the station wagon loaded and they were
off to the drug store, the grocery store, by the high school and
Richard said what are we doing here, she said Daryl wanted to get a
book, Richard said what book, it was something he wanted to read
called Lies and Deception, Richard said I'll go in with you it has been
a long time since I been in a high school, when they walked in the
door one of the student approached Richard and said hello Mr.
Thurmond and walked on by and Richard looked at Leona and said a
look a like remember. They went to the office and Richard stood in
the door way as Leona went to the receptionist desk and told her she
would like to check out a book called Lies and Deception and the
receptionist paged the librarian to let her know they were coming,
Richard stepped inside to hold the door for Leona and the
receptionist said how have you been Mike and Richard waved at her
on the way out, Leona looked at him but didn't say a word. When
they got to the library Leona told her what book she wanted and the
Liberian told her only students and the staff could check out books
and she then said I'm sorry, I didn't know you had Mike with you
and said I'll get the book for you. When Leona looked this time at
Richard, he said it's a long story, remind me to tell you about it
sometime, as the librarian handed her the book and told her to sign
the register. Leona walked by and said come on Mike we still have
some things to do, as they were leaving another student said, well
Mr. Thurmond it is so good to see you again, I hope you'll return
next year, my little sister will be in your class, if it weren't for you I
wouldn't be graduating this year. Richard told her it was good to see
her again too as she walked away, Richard said who was that girl
Leona and headed for the outside exit. Jerry was under the steering
wheel when they got back and Leona said move it buster, as she
opened the driver side door and Jerry got out of the car and got in the
back seat. Leona burnt rubber as she left the school campus and Jerry
said what's your hurry and she said I got to get Mike Thurmond to
the bank before it closes, Jerry said what's she talking about and
Leona said Jerry mind your own business. When Leona pulled into
the bank parking lot Richard said I give up what are we doing here

and she said we stopped at the bank before we went camping and Daryl went inside and was gone about fifteen minutes then we left for his dad's cabin. It was late that evening when they had arrived at the cabin, Leona got out of the car and went to the rear using a key to lower the glass in the tailgate of the station wagon and got out two Lanterns, after pumping them up she lit both of them and said what are you two waiting on , it will be close daylight be fore we get the camp set up, so you two move it and Richard said aren't we going to spend the night in the cabin and she looked at him and he said I know dumb question. It was almost a mile to the camp sight and they had to make three trips to bring all the things to the camp. When they had the tents erected, Leona said I suggest you all get some sleep breakfast will be served at seven thirty, we will be having trout, Richard said sounds good to me and Leona said I'm glad your pleased, you and Jerry has to catch them first and clean them, wake me up before you clean them, I'll get a fire started. Jerry told her if she woke him up before noon he would kill her and said if you two want fish that's fine and dandy, I'll just have some coffee when I get woke up and Leona said sure thing brother and told them good night as she went in her tent. Richard was in his element, fresh air and fly fishing nothing could suit him better, he was beside the lake as daylight broke, he had a strike as soon as his line touched the water, pulling in the largest brown trout he had ever seen and placed it in his fishing basket, within twenty minutes he caught enough trout to feed them breakfast and they all could have seconds. He had already built a fire and smelled the aroma of coffee in the air as he was cleaning the fish, when the fish were ready to eat, he woke up Leona, when she woke he was sitting on a cooler at the foot of her bed and said lady breakfast is served, holding her food said go ahead and freshen up I'll set her and serve it to you when you return, she said sure thing Daryl and walked out of the tent and then turned with tears in her eyes and said I'm so sorry Richard, he said forget it, scoot and freshen up. She came back in her tent and after she sat down he handed her a lap tray and said enjoy as he left her tent and fixed himself a plate. Jerry came from his tent and Richard said good morning sunshine as Jerry scratched himself and headed for the coffee pot. Pouring a cup of coffee Jerry said how long are we going to be here and Leona coming out of her tent replied as long as it takes. Leona asked Richard if he would like to go for a walk and Richard said no thank you I got a book I want to read and Jerry told her he would go with her and she said fine in an angry tone, Richard asked her what was wrong and she walked away like she didn't hear him and Jerry said I think its called menopause, Richard laughed and said I don't think she is quite old enough for that yet as he went to his tent laid down and started reading a book. Jerry called out to Leona and said wait up trying to run with his coffee and every now and then would say ouch that's hot. Richard had fallen asleep, he woke up and didn't hear a sound; he rose up and said Leona and didn't hear a reply. He started to get up as the book he was reading fell on the floor he bent over to pick it up and noticed a number was circled and inside the ring was the number one hundred thirty eight. He didn't think to much about it as he started walking toward the lake and saw Jerry and Leona were fly fishing on the far side of the lake, as he approached them caring a pole he said are you having any luck, just as Leona had got a trout on her hook, he was amazed at her skill with that fly rod and reached in his pocket and took out a camera just as she landed the fish he took the picture, and then he took another as she became unbalanced and fell head first into the water. He started running to her and dove into the water as she was splashing the water and when he stood up she was laughing so hard she almost was in tears, he said you idiot as he pushed her head under the water and started to walk away, and Leona jump on his back pulling him back down in the water and said its cold isn't it, helping him up and he kissed her only this time Leona didn't push him away, Jerry said will you two come out of there, your scaring the fish and the two of them ran after him as he was heading back to the camp. Leona stop and turned around and Richard said where you going she said to get Daryl's tackle box and Richard said wait up I'll go with you, stopping her started to kiss her again, only this time Leona said no, she said Richard I'm sorry I really like you but she said I'm Daryl's girl I will always be Daryl's girl, that's why I allowed you to kiss me I had to know for sure, what Daryl and I had together will last me the rest of my life and told him she was sorry if she lead him on. Richard didn't say anything just went and picked up the tackle boxes and the poles and started walking back to the camp. Leona stood there and watched him walk away she knew she had hurt him and that wasn't her intension, but she knew she had to be honest with him and herself, the only problem was most of the time she didn't know how she felt and at this point in her life, the only thing she knew was to continue with her search to find the truth of what happened to Daryl and it was destroying her a little more each day and she didn't want to face the reality that she may never find out why he was killed or prove who killed him. For the rest of the day neither one said a word to the other and Jerry spoke up, he said I have had enough, I didn't want to come here and I sure don't like camping and what's worse, I don't like to see two people who love each other destroy something over what once was, he said Leona you know you love Richard and I see Richard loves you, he said let Daryl go and she said I can't, I promised him and Jerry said what did you promise him, that you would go to the grave with him and Richard stood up and said Jerry that's quite enough, just leave her be and Leona was crying and said no Richard he is right, I do love you, I have from the first moment I saw you and its killing me inside, I can't be with you until Daryl can rest in peace , I'm all he has left, please understand, Richard told her he did understand and she wasn't alone, he said I will put Terry Myers away I promise you. Richard never tried to kiss her again he finally realized this was a one woman's man until she could put a closure on Daryl no one could get near her, he was going to be true to his word and he wouldn't rest until he saw Terry Myers, bought to justice. Richard was setting by the camp fire staring at the flames and Leona asked him if he would like a cup of coffee, and Jerry said let me get it and stumbled over a tackle box and Richard said Leona hand me that tackle box and she picked it up and handed it to him and Jerry said what you want with my tackle box and he said look and there was a number on top of it one hundred thirty eight, he walked to the tent and got the book and showed them the number telling who ever read this book he wanted to get rid of the lies and deceit and they had to use this number one hundred thirty eight, in order for him to do it. Leona said what does it mean, as Richard opened the tackle box. Inside he found a key and Jerry said I never noticed that before, Richard said Jerry what do you fish with and he pulled out a small box of flies out of his fishing vest and said these, when was the last time you opened this box he said its been years why and Richard said he needed a place to keep the key safe and knew you practically never used your tackle box and when he saw the number he couldn't resist putting it in there and then showed them the key , it was to a safety deposit box and had the number one hundred thirty eight on it. He told Leona they were leaving the next morning he said Daryl has sent them on a scavenger hunt. It was noon before they had pulled into Jerry's drive way, the bank was closed and they would half to wait until the next day to go and see what was in the safety deposit box, they were all completely exhausted by the time they put all the camping gear away and Leona told them to get some rest, she was going to return the book and take the station wagon back to her mother and told them she would fix dinner when she returned. Richard called some of his staff to give them an up date and told them all to take a few days off he would be in contact with them. When Leona returned, Jerry was already cooking dinner and told her to relax, he said his cooking wasn't the best but a least it would be filling. After dinner and the dishes were washed and put away, Richard told Leona he would see her the next morning he said he just wanted to get to the motel and get some sleep and she said there was no need for that and she said Jerry go get you an over night bag and go to mommas and we will se you in the morning, he told her he was to tried to argue and went to his bed room and got his things and left, she told Richard to take Jerry's, bed she was tied and she would see him at breakfast. Richard was in the shower when Leona woke up she smelled food and coffee brewing and was going to the kitchen and heard a knock on the door when she went to the door she saw to police officers and asked them what she could do for them. Richard was just coming out of the bedroom and saw the police and walked toward the door as Jerry was coming in be hind him, The policeman told her that her mother had collapsed and was in the hospital they tried to call but didn't receive an answer and Jerry and Leona ran to the car as Richard came in behind them and just he got to the car he told Jerry to give him the keys he was driving.

When they got to the hospital they found out her mother had had a heart stack and was in an ICU unit and was told it didn't look like she would pull through and they told Leona and Jerry to follow them and Richard sat down in the waiting room. Four hours had past when Leona and Jerry returned to the waiting room Jerry had his arm around Leona as she was crying her heart out and Richard stood up and walked to her, she looked at him and said she is going to be fine. Leona told him to go ahead and go to the bank she wanted to stay with her mother and Jerry told him he wasn't leaving either and Richard said the bank will keep I am staying with you. It was four days later when the three of them walked out of the hospital, Leona's mother was going to be released the next day and Leona wanted everything ready for her when she returned home, Jerry said he would have a nurse with her around the clock for the next couple of weeks and told Leona to go home and take a bath and do something with her hair, she was a mess and it was Jerry who sat there four days with out taking a bath, Richard had called one of his staff to bring them some clothes, but Jerry refused to change he said they were his lucky clothes, he had them on when his mom pulled through and he was leaving them on until they released her and Richard told him just to stay down wind from them. Richard and Leona dropped Jerry off at his home and they proceeded to the bank, Richard told Leona he didn't know what was in their safety deposit box and she would half to get the contents out of it alone and she told Richard she had never seen the safety deposit box she just went in the bank to sign the paper where she could, get in it, Daryl always went to the bank alone. When they went in the bank Leona told them she wanted a bag to put some things in and then went to the vault, when she opened the safety deposit box, she didn't look what was in it, she just put every thing in a bag, when she came out her and Richard went to the car. They returned to Jerry's home and went into Leona's office she took everything out of the bag; she saw an envelope with her name written on it, she opened the envelope and started crying and handed it to Richard, as Richard read the letter out loud, it said My darling wife; if you're reading this letter I know you are safe, all through are marriage I never kept anything from you, I am sorry that I had to put you through this, but there was no other way I could do it and keep you safe. A secrete I kept from you all these years, has come back to haunt me, but I knew I couldn't tell you until now, I promised a friend many years ago that I wouldn't tell his secrete to any one and I never broke my promise, only he has gone completely crazy, he knew if I told, you would have called the police and if you had, you wouldn't be reading this now, I don't think I'll ever get to return to you my darling, I am only going to tell you this much, just in case I manage to return, this is why I am giving you clues where to look, in the hope, you will be completely out of danger, if I should not return, they will lead you to who is responsible, my only hope is you don't discover the truth, before I do what I know is best for you, mom and dad. I love you my darling and I will until my last breath, you have always been the love of my life, my hope, my dreams, my guiding light, that holds onto my very soul, be safe, I adore you "Daryl" Go to the hide a rock. Leona was trying to fight back the tears as she said I love you to my precious, Richard wanted desperately to comfort her but thought he would be stepping out of bounds, and knew she would make the first move if she wanted him to do so. Leona said Richard I don't remember how to go to the hide a rock, he only took me here once, It was right after we were married, it was his special place, where he put things that was most valuable to him, it was his secrete place, Richard what am I going to do she asked. Richard said go on vacation what else, he said I am taking you away for a couple of weeks to clear your mind, I don't want you to even think about anything, he said you name the place you would like to go and I'll take you, any where in the world and I'll call my sister Lindsey to take care of you, just the three of us, what do you think. She said what about mother and he said you know that Jerry is going to have a nurse for her twenty four seven, and if you want to come back an hour after we leave I'll bring you, you just say the word I am at you beck and call. She said what about the investigation he said unless you can remember there is no investigation. Leona started clearing her desk and after she put everything away she said call your sister. He said I'll do it right now and he called Lindsey, when he finished talking to her, he said she will be here tonight and we will leave first thing in the morning and Leona said fine, I just want to make sure mom is alright before we leave and Richard said it sounds like a plan. Leona decided they would go to New Mexico and hang out on a dude ranch and Richard said that's fine and the next morning the were off to New Mexico, they went to a ranch called Boots and Saddles and Leona told Richard she wasn't filling well she told him and Lindsey to go for a ride, when they got back if she was filling better she would go to lunch with them. Richard and Lindsey left a half hour later and Leona called a cab and decided she was gone to Glenn Dale, New Mexico she called a cab and had him take her to a car rental she new she had to hurry Richard would be back off there ride in two hours, Leona rented her car and she had a hundred mile drive to Glenn Dale after two and a half hours she drove into Glenn Dale, she went to a pawn shop to buy her a gun and enough ammunition to go practice with before she went looking for Terry, she drove about three miles out of town, pulled the car over by the side of the road and set up a soda can to shoot at, after missing it a half dozen times she finally hit and shot again to make sure it wasn't just a lucky shot, again she hit the can. she was only about fifteen feet from the can then she move back about twenty feet and shot and hit the can four times in a row she worked her way back to fifty feet and shot missing the can then she tried again hitting it this time and she thought to her self she was ready to face him. She got back in her car and drove to the high school and found it closed and she went to a pay phone to look up a listing for him and found out by the address that was given, he lived ten miles out of town. Stopping to inquire where his residence was after not being able to find the road, she was told she had passed the road and was told to make a right turn on it and he lived in a farm house that had tar paper brown brick siding on it. Leona got in her car and was headed out of town when she saw a car coming up fast behind her she started driving faster and finally she had enough, she pulled over to the side of the road got out of her car and started shooting and then she heard Richard shouting don't shot its me, she asked him what he was doing there and he said I had you followed I thought you might be up to something nutty, she said go away Richard I cant remember where the hide a rock is and he isn't going to get away with killing my husband so just leave, Richard said this is not the way and she said you told me if I couldn't remember, the case was over, it may be over for you but not me I loved Daryl and if you can't understand that, then its to bad, this is my last warning Richard leave and he started walking toward her and she shot him in the leg, she said don't make me kill you and he kept coming and she kept shooting and finally he took the gun from her hand and she said I hate you and got in her car and drove off. Leona drove the rest of that day, and through the night only stopping for fuel, she was two hundred miles out of Ellisville when she pulled into a motel and got a room. It was midnight when Leona woke up still shaking inside and her tears turned to anger she finally cried it all out and thought to herself, I will kill him if it's the last thing I do, she got back into her car and thought about the last twelve years hoping to find the man and he is still walking free and Leona was determined he wasn't going to stay that way. Leona was in such a deep thought she didn't realize she was just outside of Ellisville; she decided she would turn her car in and call Jerry to come and get her. Jerry was picking her up about forty five minutes later and he told her Richard had called and by the way he is alright and Leona said I wouldn't care if he were dead. Jerry said Leona you know you don't mean that she said of course I do if he cared for me he would have already killed Terry Myers, Jerry was pulling up in his drive way and Richard pulled in behind him and Leona told him to get all his stuff out of her office, she said I'll take care of that killer myself since your not man enough to. Richard told her if she left Ellisville he would have her locked up and said if I see you here again it one be your leg I'll put a bullet into are we clear and she went to her office and stated throwing out all the papers and Richard said go ahead I have the originals then Leona lit a match setting them on fire as Jerry ran to get a water hose saying, have you gone crazy get your things out of my house and stay away, that hurt Leona but she said fine I'll be out within the hour. Leona called a cab when she got her things and Richard asked her where she was going and she said to finish what I started. The cab driver put her things in the cab and Leona told him to drive. Leona's car was at her mothers and she went there and put her thing in her car and then went to see her mother. Her mother was very pleased to see Leona and asked her to join her for dinner, Leona was quiet though dinner and her mom asked her what was on her mind and she said nothing mom I'm fine and smiled got up and kissed her moms forehead and said I'll be gone a while mom and I'll keep in touch. Before her mom could ask where she was going Leona went out the front door and went to her car, she got in and drove off as she was heading out of town the police pulled her over and ask where she was headed and she told them she was going home, they said it better be in Ellisville and she said I live in Nebraska, look at my tags, the officer said well I didn't have that understanding, I sure can't stop you from going home and told her she was free to go. Leona was determined to bring her husbands killer to justice as she drove out of town, she had a hard time concentrating on the road, her mind kept wondering off thinking about the pictures she saw of Daryl lying in his own blood not having anyone to help, she thought if he had just told her, she at least could have been with him and would have gladly died beside him and started crying thinking of what he must have went through facing that psychopath alone. Fear came over her something she had never had before, this time she was alone, going against everything she had been taught, knowing if she faced this man she would kill him or die trying. Leona started filling sick inside, she had only driven a hundred miles and she felt as if she had been up for days, she keep fighting the felling she had to turn around and go back to where she knew she would be safe. The words keep flowing into her head if you can't remember there is no investigation, she felt so helpless yet she wasn't going to stop, she drove for hours going through states until she reached a point of exhaustion. Leona decided to stop at Shreveport Louisiana and rest a few days before she went on to New Mexico. She had to remove this filling of fear from her body and went to a liquor store and bought several bottles of whiskey, she went to a hotel and paid for a room for a week and then as she went inside her room unwrapped a plastic cup and filled it full of whiskey then turned it up and drank it all down, she kicked of her shoes and turned the television on as she poured another glass of whiskey turned it up and drank it down and decided she would try to get some rest as she got undresses, she was walking toward the bath room, finding herself waking up the next morning with a splitting headache. Wondering what she was doing on the floor and how she got there, remember the liquor store and drinking on an empty stomach. She went straight to the whiskey bottle and didn't wait to use a glass and put the bottle to her lips and started gulping it down, when she sat it down it was empty. She got undressed walked through the room naked and went to the shower and put her head under it and stood there in the hot stream of water until the cold water hit her body then she turned it off and walked back into the room and opened another bottle and started drinking on it after about an hour she got dressed and decided to go get something to eat and she drank the last of the bottle sat it down and walked outside her room and got in her car and drove to a little restaurant not far from the hotel. She went inside and ordered breakfast only eating a few bites went back to her car and back to the motel and started drinking more, she completely drank to more bottles and fell back on her bed and didn't wake up until the next morning and she was sick enough to die as she went to the bath room and got rid of everything that was inside her. She put a cold compress on her head looked at her last bottle of whiskey got up took the lid off and poured it down the sink. She then went and took a long hot bath and got dressed, went to her car and headed back to the interstate and was on her way to New Mexico again. She had only driven about fifty miles and stopped to get coffee and to fill her car with gasoline, she went to the rest room and looked in the mirror and started laughing she had forgot to comb her hair and it was standing straight up. She comb her hair and decided she was stupid going after this killer and didn't know how to defend her self so she decided to go to Dallas and take a course on self defense and learn the proper way to handle a gun. She said he has lived this long a few more days is not going to make a difference one way or the other and she only had about two hundred miles before she would get into Dallas, Texas. The more she thought about Terry the angrier she got and the more angrier she got the faster she would drive having the music turned so loud it was deafening, fighting traffic that was heavy so it took her almost five hours to get to Dallas. She went to a roadside park and walked through the tall grass on an embankment thinking things over in her mind she wanted to be absolutely sure this was the plan she wanted to follow, she stood and watched cars come and go out of the park, she saw men with their wives and watched as some would taunt each other playing and would smile when she remembered how her and Daryl would do a lot of the same things she saw others doing, for the next hour she played out the events in her life that made her the happiest and everything she thought of Daryl was included.

It was like she never knew any other happiness except when she and Daryl were together, looking at her reflection in a small pond noticed once more the thing that made her happy was missing.

She became outraged with hatred and all she could think about was killing Terry Myers as she went to a phone book to find a place that could give her a crash course in self defense.

Leona would look for someone who could teach her how to use a gun.

She went to the yellow pages looking for adds that read "learn self defense" she managed to find one the ad commented anyone interested should call Robert Sterling, she dialed a number a made an appointment to see him that after noon and she heard her stomach growling and knew she had to get something to eat.

After she had lunch she went to see Robert, from the awards he had in martial arts she knew she had come to the right man and the first thing he asked her was why she wanted to learn self defense and she replied for self preservation and he just laughed and asked her when she wanted to start and she replied immediately.

She told Robert her time was limited she could only give him a couple of days to tech her and he answered her saying "that's impossible!" and looking disappointed told him she was sorry she wasted his time and got up from her chair, he said if you tell me the real reason you want to do this I'll see what I can do and she said I am going to kill a man and I need to live long enough to do it.

He told her he would teach her only she would have to give him three to four and she replied in one condition, he told her to go on and she replied you'll have to teach me how to handle a gun to.

He told her that was not going to be a problem.

Robert told her to come with him and she followed him out the door and he told his secretary to cancel all his classes for awhile that he was going on vacation and wasn't certain how long he would be gone.

He looked at Leona saying lets go and she asked where was it they were going and he answered does it matter and told her to follow him, they drove for about an hour and he pulled into a dirt road.
Robert took her to a place that looked like some kind of temple.
He parked his car, sat there for a moment opened his car door saying we are here and she asked him what is this place and he smiled saying, the place you will learn to live, she snapped at him saying "just what does that suppose top mean!' He replied to her remarking that she had already died she would have to learn how to live before he could teach her how to defend herself.
When they walked into the building they were greeted by a beautiful Japanese woman and he introduced this woman as Sue Ling his wife, he told his wife to get her dressed and prepare her for battle and his wife told her to follow her.
Robert left the room and Sue Ling told her to strip and Leona looked at her saying forget it lady she didn't come there for a kinky weekend, Sue Ling didn't like what she had implied then told Leona they had to prepare that they were in a place for her to learn the art of survival and any more out burst like that she could leave.
Leona done as she was asked and they both went down into a bath that looked like milk, Leona told Sue Ling it was to hot, the woman smiled then sat down and told her to sit it would only take a few seconds to get use to it, Leona sat down and the woman told her to close her eyes and to relax.
Leona thought how good this felt as she found herself wanting to fall to sleep.
About twenty minutes later the woman told her she was ready to get dressed and handed her a towel as she came out of the murky water, she said here is your Karate gi, put this on.
She helped Leona get dressed saying now we go to my husband, and Leona followed her as she went out into a court yard and walked by a fountain that had gold fish in it and saw Robert sitting on a mat.
When they walked on the mat Sue Ling bowed to her husband and then to Leona and walked away.
He asked Leona if she found the bath relaxing and Leona answered saying it was nice and thanked him, he asked her if she were ready to get started, she replied yes as he threw her down on the mat.

He told her that was her first lesson not to trust anyone.
Leona got to her feet and hit him beside his head saying she didn't,
he threw her back down on the mat and replied good, now are you
ready to learn he asked and she replied well of course and got back to
her feet.
He told her not to face some one straight on to stand side ways this
way she would make her self a smaller target, he taught her moves in
aikido and how to take a man down by using hand control if some
one should grab her clothing from the front.
Only he made her fell the pain as he was instructing her and told her
to quit anytime she liked, if she had to face an opponent she better
get use to it, he showed her how to get away from someone who
snuck up behind her.
Using her body as a counter weight could easily throw an opponent
to the ground, after a four hour session his wife came to get her to
freshen up before dinner. Leona was served very little food and
Robert told her he wanted her to lose weight.
He told her he didn't have time for her to lose the weight gradually
and he wanted her body to be in tip top shape, Leona thought that
they were finished for the day, every bone in her body ached and
Robert told her they had to work out four more hours before she
could rest.
Leona was leaning fast that she hated this man, but knew if she
wanted to have a chance to survive long enough to kill Terry Myers,
she had to listen to him. Leona couldn't hardly walk after there last
session was over but she was determined she was going to learn
every thing he could teach her.
It seemed like Leona had no longer lain down that night when Sue
Ling was waking her and helping her get ready for that day, after her
bath Sue Ling gave her a message and Leona was thinking and asked
herself why she hadn't ever had a massage before, she felt like she
had died and gone to heaven.
When Sue Ling took her to her husband she stayed ten feet away
from him it was to early in the morning to land on her fanny and she
never took her eyes off him, Robert told her to follow him as he
walked out of the court yard and told her to go in a room and put
some sweet close on.

Leona went in and hurried getting dressed, she didn't know if he would try to attack her in the dressing room or not and then she ran out the door keeping her eyes on him, while she put her tennis shoes on and he told her to try to keep up.

Leona went at him full force bringing her body in the air kicking him beside his head and when her body touched the ground she sprang up and attacked him again, only this time he was ready for her catching her in midair and threw her to the ground and he turned and started running across the field in the back of his house.

They ran for three miles and came to a shooting range and Robert told Leona his brother was a police officer and he would be giving her a few lessons on how to handle a gun, he told her to do exactly as she was told his brother lacked patience.

Leona asked him where he thought he was going and his brother replied any where he pleases now follow me while he finished his run.

After a half hour on teaching safety the instructor took her on the firing range and they walked fifteen yards from the target, that was a silhouette of a man, he walked up and told her where all the kill areas was and told her they would get started then walked back to the fifteen yard line.

He told her to lock and load and then said get ready on the firing line, aim then said fire, when she finished she kept the nozzle of the gun down field, put the gun on safety then handed it to the instructor, they the proceeded to the target and the instructor was impressed with her results, marking the bullet holes, he looked at her saying lets see what you can do from twenty five yards.

When they went to the twenty five yard line he followed the same procedure and again he was impressed, then it was time for the fifty yard line and he went over the same procedure again and Leona got excited and he took the gun from her hand and scolder her saying this is not a game.

They went back to the target and Leona only hit it twice, once in the leg and once on the elbow.

When she turned she saw Robert waiting on her and the instructor told her it was time to go and she would have one last chance to do it right and told her to get off his field, she looked at him smiled walked up to threw him to the ground.

Leona didn't like his attitude but thought what the hay, he is just doing his job as she walked up to Robert and threw him on the ground and took off running, by the end of the week Leona had been taught all Robert could teach her in the amount of time he was given. Leona was given a certificate from her shooting instructor, with her class marked as Marksman.

She wrote Robert a check and told him to follow her to the bank she would get it cashed for him if he liked and he told her that wasn't necessary and tore up the check telling her he didn't do her any favors by teaching her and handed her a bullet proof vest.

Robert made her promise him she wouldn't face him without it, he told her it may be the edge she needed to survive and she hugged his wife Sue Lings neck thanking them both for all their help as she got into her car to drive away.

Leona was thinking how nice it was of him to have her car brought to her and allowing her to live after the way she acted during instruction using his groin for a punching bag and him almost giving her punch to her head that would have killed her if he had followed through.

Leona had purchased a nine millimeter pistol from her instructor with a spring loaded shoulder holster and within the hour she knew she would be back on the interstate going to New Mexico with vengeance on her mind.

Leona had to know for sure what she learned, would give her a chance of survival and going into a redneck bar would soon find out if she could handle herself or not, Leona was determined she would tick of the ugliest, meanest looking man in the bar and hoped she could handle herself if he decided to use her head for a punching bag.

It didn't take her long to find the one she was looking for, in Leona's mined they all looked like that when they came from the back woods of no where and every one of them acted like they were the meanest ambries in Dallas.

Leona soon found out the women that were with them thought they were too and the party began, after Leona told the man he looked like a big sissy and he shouldn't bring his sister to a public place they were hog pins for folks like them.

Well she had said pretty much all she needed to as she broke a beer bottle over his head and caught the ladies arm trying to slice her face with a razor knife putting her on top of the big man that was laying unconscious on the floor.

Holding the razor at her throat Leona told her, it was her lucky day as she kicked her beside her head and turned to walk out the door and the meanest man in the place just happened to be standing in the door way asking her why she was in such a big hurry.

He told Leona he would sure like a big kiss from her before she left and she said sure thing pinky and kicked him as if he were a football, taking his breath away and it wasn't from her beauty.

She stepped on his back on the way out the door saying you all have a fine day you hear.

Leona had a ten hour drive ahead of her and was obeying every speed limit she assumed Richard would try to have her stopped.

Leona arrived in Glenn dale, New Mexico at ten pm that evening she was headed straight for Terries home only this time she wasn't going to be stopped and took a different route that she would half to drive double the distance and if she has her way Terry would be dead before morning.

She drove by his house and seen the lights were still on and she decided she would find a place to hide her car.

She dove nearly two miles before she found a side road pulling into the road she noticed an abanded house and pulled her car in behind it, she put the bullet proof vest on and then put on her shoulder holster and paced her gun in the holster after cocking it and putting it on safety.

Then she put on a dark colored jacket and started running down the road toward Terry's house, she was there in twenty minutes, as she creep up to peek in the window, she saw Terry sitting on a sofa watching TV.

She started to work her way up to another window, when she felt a hand coming beside her cheek and threw the man over her shoulder striking him with her gun and she saw it was Richard lying unconscious.

She reached down and got him under his arms and started dragging him into a cluster of trees and just as she got him there, she saw Terry walk out on the porch, as someone turned a light on and said do you see anything and he said no.

Leona already had her gun out taking aim as he stepped back in side the house, Richard was coming around and she decided to leave before he got up and she took off running down the road and when she made it back to her car, she opened the door and waited until day light and thought she would give it another try.

Only this time she was going to pull into his drive way and try to get a shot at him, at this point she thought she had nothing to lose.

Leona had dozed off and when she woke up it was already 7:30 am, she started the car and was headed back to Terry's house, she thought to herself if Richard interfered he better kill her that would be the only way he could stop her.

When she got back to Terry's house she seen his car was already gone but that didn't mean he wasn't still at home.

Leona pulled up in his drive way and said to herself its now or never and got out of her car and walked up and knocked on the door and stood and waited, but no one answered, she took out her pistol and started knocking a gain.

Then she walked to the window on the side of the house and peeked in, there was no one there she went to the side door and kicked the door in and went inside looking in every room.

She had tears in her eyes saying this is for you Daryl as she pulled out a can of blood red paint and spayed the word crimson on every wall in the house, in her mind it was like setting the house on fire, lighting it in ever room.

Leona wanted Terry to know she knew that he had killed Daryl and he was going to be destroyed as she walked out and went to her car, got in and headed for a little town nearby.

Leona knew that Richard would be looking for her car, so she parked hers and she rented one to go to Glendale, she took the alternate route back to Glendale plotting in her mind as she drove.

The only place she knew to look was at the school.

She decided she would go and get some breakfast and go by the school at dinner time hoping to catch him outside, Leona was setting a few blocks from the school and waited until she thought every one would be outside and then made her move.

She pulled up in the parking lot of the school, waiting for him to show his face.

She could visualize Daryl laying in his blood only about forty feet from where she was parked and finally she saw Terry, as she got out of her car, she was going to call to him to see if she could lure him to her.

She had got almost out of the parking lot while she kept an eye on him, she was in range but there were too many high school kids in his area, so she waited to get a clear shot, visualizing him in her mind falling to the ground dead.

He stood there like he knew someone was watching him, as she watched his head move back and forth and in a couple on moments, a woman and two children were walking to him.

Leona watched him as he reached for the little boy, picking him up; she stood there, wanting to kill him then and there not wanting to wait for another moment, only she knew she couldn't kill him in front of the children.

She thought to herself who is this woman, why don't she leave, Leona walked across the street and walked toward him as he played with the little boy, she walked up to him and made a comment saying cute kid.

Leona stared at him, as he tried to figure out who she was and she looked at him and it was all she could do was to say to him, "this is your lucky day!" flashing her gun at him as she turned to walk away going back to her car hoping he would come after her as she glanced over her shoulder and saw him standing there as if he were in a trance.

Leona got in her car and left.

Terry was looking at her as she crossed the street and remembered her from the motel in Chicago where he tried to lure her to a restaurant and smiled as her car started to go by, he knew she would be watching for him to follow her and he also knew where she lived.

He didn't consider her to be a threat to him and thought to himself she did have lots of nerve, but if she figured out what had happened she couldn't prove it or she would already tried to have him arrested.

Leona knew she could go back home now, she didn't care that he might figure out who she was and come looking for her, she would be ready and waiting, she would give him as much of a chance, that he had given Daryl.

Finally she wasn't afraid any more and she smiled as she returned the rental car and got in her own car saying "Ellisville I am coming home!", she thought this time he knew she came to kill him and if her hunch was right he would be coming after her, if not she would come back.

Leona left the rental car lot and headed for Terry's house she figured she might get another chance to kill him and hope he would return home, she wanted to see his face when he saw his house was no longer a safe place to be.

In her mind she could see it burn to the ground.

She slowly drove up to where he lived, she pulled to the side of the road and she saw a police car was setting in the drive way and a woman standing at their car pointing to the house as the woman got in their car.

Leona watched the police car back out of the drive way, she slid down in her seat and watched as they headed toward Glendale, Leona went back to the abanded house and parked her car and decided to get some sleep it was going to be a long night.

What she was going to do she would need all the rest she could muster.

Leona woke up at eight thirty that evening got a beverage out of a cooler; she set and contemplated how she was going to go about killing the monster that lured her husband to him.

Leona got out of the car and started running down the road toward his home and saw a police car in the drive way and Terry coming out of the house with a suit case, all Leona could do was stand and watch as they left the premises.

She knew the last chance she had was gone and now it was his turn to stock her if he wanted and she only hoped he would, one way or the other one of them would die and it didn't matter to Leona, witch way it turned out, life as she knew it was already a thing of the past and her future was nothing but emptiness.

When the police car had past her she quickly ran to her car getting in it, she came out on the highway as if she had went mad, she turned the wheels on her car turning it around and headed for the police car, in a matter of minutes she had caught up to them.

She came upon the police car ramming into the back of it and shoving her foot down on the accelerator, Leona was acting as though something inside her had snapped as she shoved the police car over the embankment, quickly she stopped her car and as she got to the bank she saw that Terry had shot and killed the policeman throwing his gun on the front seat of the police car as he heard the pistol fire coming from Leona's pistol.

He started to run inside the woods when one of Leona's bullets had penetrated his arm knocking him down and he got up and started running again as he saw her come over the embankment.

Leona went in the woods looking for him saw a large blood spot at the edge of the river and could see where he had jumped in the water and knew as swift as the current was there was no way she could find him then proceeded back to her car.

On her walk back she could visualize him drowning but knew he was a powerful swimmer in collage and won several tournaments even won a bronze medal during the Olympics, Daryl would tell her stories about Terry, she knew he could be a little nutty at time but would have been the last person she would have thought would have killed Daryl.

Leona finally made it back to the road and got in her car and drove away, she had went to a pay phone calling the police and told them she had saw Terry kill the policeman, that they had ran off the road and she thought maybe he was hurt he was holding his shoulder as he had went into the woods then she hung up the phone.

Leona started on her trip home, hoping to get some kind of peace of mind before she got there.

Leona took her time getting back to Ellisville, she started felling good about herself, she started to sing again as she used to and knew Daryl would be proud of her.

Leona had saw a lake and thought she would go there to get her thoughts together, she was getting some peace back in her life, she saw a sign saying get back to nature and said what an idea as she drove to the lake stopping at a tour guides office and hired a guide to take her pike fishing.

This is something she had always wanted to do and she thought now was as good as any time to go, it had been a long time since she had wanted to do anything and was looking forward to this day of fishing.

She just wanted to get her mind completely off everything, the guide she had was a perfect gentleman something she always appreciated in a man and he put her on the best fishing she had in years.

She really hated for the day to end, but all things in life comes to an end at some point and she figured she would just get in her car and drive most of the way home then spend the night at a motel and be on her way early the next morning.

It was four days later, as she was driving hwy 219, going into Ellisville, she noticed a mile marker, one hundred thirty eight, she rubbed her eyes and she couldn't believe what she had just seen.

It was as if Daryl was marking a trail for her to follow and when she looked, she saw a sign saying Ellisville and Elkins, she remembered where the hide a rock was saying to herself, why didn't I think of this before and then she started driving to the town of Elkins.

She was going to a farm that belonged to Daryl's grand parents, Leona hadn't thought about his grand parents in years, she only had met his grandmother once at a nursing home and only visited the farm once, she remembered telling Daryl that Elkins was an odd name for a town.

It took her about an hour to drive and when she looked she was only was driving twenty five miles per hour, she pulled up in the drive way of the farm, it had been twenty five years since she had been there, the house was almost completely gone.

Leona got out of the car and walked upon the hill side of the farm, she had forgotten how pretty this farm was and thought it was a shame no one chose to build on it.

When she reached the top of the hill, she closed her eyes and was just standing there trying to think where the hide a rock was, what was it Daryl had said, she stood their trying to visualize in her mind what he said to her and didn't see the other car pull in the drive way and she heard a voice calling out, but couldn't understand what was being said. In a few minutes it became clear who was there, as Richard started walking up the hill with a bad leg and a band around his head, the hill was almost to much for him and he said, is this the place and Leona said yes it was and she said I think we need to go over to the other side, its been so long I lost my bearings.

As they stated walking across the side of the hill her memory came back to her, as if it were yesterday, it is a hundred and thirty eight steps from that tree to the cluster of rocks that was what Daryl said for her to remember.

She started stepping it off, when she had got to one hundred and thirty eight she turned and climb on top of a cluster of rock, removing several and said I found it, I found the hide a rock and bent over to pick it up.

When she looked inside there was another note, saying it's in the bee hive.

Now this clue was easy, she knew just where to look and told Richard we better get going, we need to go to Beverly, Richard asked what else is in that thing and she brought out a huge marble, called a cat eye, a toy solider and some bubble gum wrappers and he said what in the world did he want with those, she said you're a little dumb huh, his favorite jokes are on the wrappers.

She said knock, knock and Richard said whose there she said she said boo and he said boo who and she said your crying.

Richard replied that was a knee slapper and Leona made an awkward face saying just how old are you.

Richard just started walking down the hill, it was an hour later when they drove into Beverly and Leona turned down a side street and pulled in front of a house, she got out of her car, walked up to the front porch.

Leona then looked in the bee hive and found a key with a note attached, the note was faded out, a woman came out on the porch and said Leona how good to see you and Leona said it had been awhile.

The woman saw she had something in her hand and asked what do you have there and she said a key, out of your bee hive, Daryl put it in there for me.

She commented he was a strange kid, but I always liked him and Leona said you should his your nephew and she said I know it, when he put that key in there, he told me not two read the note, after he left I did anyway and Leona said what did it say, she said it was strange, it said look in dads desk, a ledger.

Richard thought it was kind of weird to have a bee hive on the porch, but didn't even ask why it was there.

The woman told Leona curiosity had got the best of her and she called him later and ask him what it meant and he told me, he was in a hurry and it was none of my business, you know, it took some nerve for him to hang up on me like that.

Leona told Daryl aunt she would love to talk, but they had to go and said bye, as she was getting in her car.

Leona drove back to Jerry's and asked him if he was still angry and he answered at what then she kissed him, she went in the house and ask him to bring in her luggage.

When he and Richard came in the house, Leona was taking a shower after an hour, she came out dressed to the tee and Richard asked where are we going, she replied not we, me, I going to Daryl's moms house and Jerry told her they were on vacation and won't be back for two weeks and she asked him how did he know that and he answered saying, she called, she always does when they leave town, it sort of makes me responsible to watch there house, a job that should be yours I might add he told Leona.

Leona asked Jerry where the key was to their house and Jerry said under the flower pot, on the windowpane and she said thanks and started walking out the door and said aren't you coming Richard.

He just shook his head and walked out the door.

Leona and Richard walked down the street.

Daryl's parents only lived a block away from Jerry, Leona walk around the house to the back door, reached up and lifted the flower pot and removed the key, unlocked the door and put the key back.

She went to the front door and let Richard in and told him to go with her, she walked through the house and into Daryl's dad's bed room, walked over to the desk, pulling it out from the wall.

Richard said what are you doing and she said I'm going to unlock the desk and Richard seen a key slot in back of the desk and heard a click when she turned the key, Leona said cool huh.

When Daryl built the desk he figured it would be better if everyone couldn't see where to unlock the desk and had a locking devise made, where he could lock it from the back, anyone trying to open the drawer, would think they were fake.

Leona went to the front of the desk pulled out the drawer and picked up a ledger, she opened the Ledger and seen a note and it said turn to page one hundred thirty eight, Richard was looking over her shoulder and said he really liked that number.

Leona started to read then stopped wiping the tears from her eyes, she handed the ledger to Richard and he started to read it and Leona suggested he read it to her and Richard replied alright here it goes.

My Dearest Leona if you are reading this ledger, this means I have been killed, I am Flying to New Mexico to meet with Terry Myers, he said if I didn't come he would kill everyone in my family and I can't allow that to happen.

Leona I know it has to be you reading this I never told mom and dad about the drawers, I told them I built the desk this way so it would look like it had drawers, now I am glad I did.

I didn't know Terry had killed his wife, to collect on the Insurance policy I sold him while we were in collage; he was secretly married and asked me to swear I wouldn't tell this secret to anyone.

Her name is Susan Livingston, her Parent lives at fourteen, Mocking Byrd Lane, in Elkins, West Virginia, he told me if his parents found out he was married, they wouldn't pay his tuition.

There is a copy of the insurance papers in the bottom drawer of the desk, his brother Phil told me about his wife Breanne dieing and I called him to give my condolences, it was then I knew he was crazy, he thought I knew he was a bigamist and said I only wanted to black mail him.

He told me he had killed Susan to pay off some debts and to buy a new car to impress his other wife Breanne and asked me how I found out that he poised Breanne; I tried to tell him I didn't know.

He said well you do now, I asked him why he did it; he said she had lied to him and got pregnant and said she knew he didn't want children.

Daryl told Leona he never dreamed that by calling a friend, it would lead to this, saying he was truly sorry, there is a phone tape recording of our conversation in my Guitar; I knew you used to try to play it every now and then and I hoped you would find it.

I don't know what this means, he told me he had both of them on ice.

Richard told Leona that was all he had written.

Leona said lets go and get his Guitar and nail that whacko, Richard told her to lead the way, Richard carried the ledger and had removed the Insurance papers from the other drawer and they walked back to Jerry's house.

Leona and Richard drove to her mother's house and Leona went into the garage and carried out a guitar case, she then opened it and busted the guitar on the driveway and picked up the phone tape.

She said lets go listen to the tape, they went in her mothers house and the nurse said her mother was asleep.

Leona went into the living room, followed by Richard and put the phone tape in the phone, pressed play and they listened, while this mad man talked to her husband and at the end, heard her husbands voice say, he would be on the next flight out.

Richard said he must have worked all night in order to leave all this evidence.

Richard told Leona there was only one thing that bothered him, how did Daryl get the money to buy that huge boat, Leona told him that was simple he was left a trust fund by his Grandfather and he could spend it anyway he liked once he reached the age of twenty five.

Didn't you notice he only made payments for a year and they were a hundred and fifty dollars a month, Leona told him he was a little slow for being such a smart man, she knew that right off.

Richard chuckled saying how could I have possibly known that, she replied you saw his payments, did you really think he could have a boat like that boat for that amount of money, remember you never asked, typical for a man she remarked.

Richard and Leona went to the police with all the evidence Daryl had left them and Terry Myers was picked up for murder, they found the bodies of both women in a freezer in a storage building at his girl friends house.

She swore she didn't know they were in there, after extensive questioning they determined she was telling the truth and no charges were brought against her.

The trial lasted four months and Terry Myers, was found guilty on all three murders and was given three consecutive lifetime sentences.

Terry Myers was found dead in his cell, one hundred thirty eight days after he was convicted.

He was hanging by the neck, with a note pinned to his chest, all that was written on the note, was the word "crimson", that had been written a hundred and thirty eight times. Charges were bought up against Leona and Richard after an inmate said he saw them give envelopes to some of the guards; the inmate was killed shortly after he gave testimony against them.

All charges were dropped for the lack of evidence. Richard and Leona were married a year later, in the parking lot of the Glenn Dale, New Mexico high school, were Daryl was killed. Leona said, if she could marry Richard there, she knew Daryl would finally be at rest and his presence would be with her.

Jerry said she been hanging out with Fanny to long and was starting to get a little loony, after the ceremony, Leona gave Richard his first wedding present, she handed him the title to the boat that Daryl bought for her and had it signed over to him.

When they went to the gulf coast He found a note from Leona saying take me fishing. Richard was thinking to himself, what a honey moon, perfect for any man.

Richard gave her his first wedding present, a bill for one hundred thirty eight dollars for services rendered, she asked him why that amount, and he said it just was a catchy number in more ways than one.

He told Leona to pay him a dollar a year, as they got in Leona's car. When they were driving away in Leona's car the license plate read, THE END

www.ingramcontent.com/pod-product-compliance
Lightning Source LLC
Chambersburg PA
CBHW031114260626
47172CB00001B/363